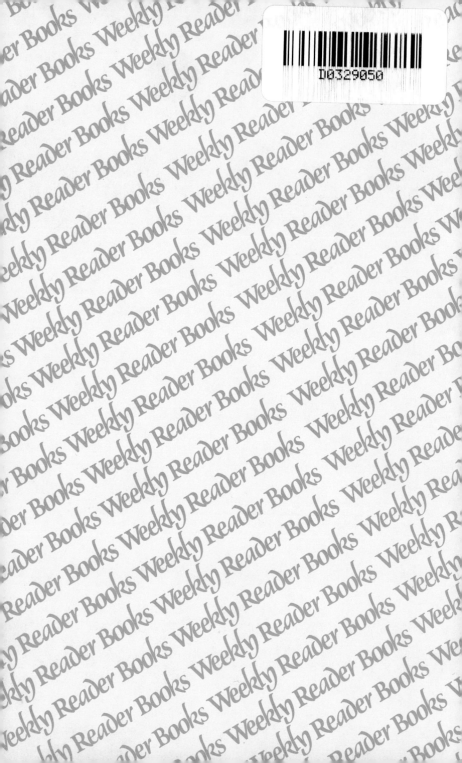
D0329050

The Ghost Upstairs

WEEKLY READER BOOKS presents

THE GHOST UPSTAIRS

by
Lila Sprague
McGinnis

Illustrated
by Amy Rowen

HASTINGS HOUSE

NEW YORK 10016

Copyright © 1982 by Lila Sprague McGinnis

All rights reserved. No part of this publication may be
reproduced, stored in a retrieval system, or transmitted,
in any form or by any means, electronic, mechanical,
photocopying, recording or otherwise, without the prior
permission of the copyright owner or the publishers.

Library of Congress Cataloging in Publication Data

McGinnis, Lila Sprague.
    The ghost upstairs.

    Summary: Albert has difficulties explaining his
sudden neatness and better grades, but who would
believe him if he revealed that a twelve-year-old
ghost who "can't abide a mess" has moved into his
room?
    [1. Ghosts—Fiction]   I. Rowen, Amy, ill.   II. Title.
PZ7.M16775Gh 1982   [Fic]   81-20337
ISBN 0-8038-2716-4   AACR2

Published simultaneously in Canada by
Saunders of Toronto, Ltd., Don Mills, Ontario

Printed in the United States of America

This book is a presentation of
Weekly Reader Books.

Weekly Reader Books offers book clubs for children
from preschool through junior high school.

For further information write to:
Weekly Reader Books
1250 Fairwood Ave.
Columbus, Ohio 43216

Edited for Weekly Reader Books
and published by arrangement
with Hastings House.

Contents

The Ghost Upstairs

Chapter 1

Ghostly Guests

Albert wasn't expecting a ghost that April afternoon. He cleared a space on his desk and worked three long division problems. Then he stretched his arms high in the air.

Someone said, "Oooof!"

Albert whirled around. No one here but himself, and he hadn't said anything. The disc jockey, he thought. He looked toward the radio. It floated up and over the top bunk.

"What is this thing?" a voice asked.

Weird prickles crawled up Albert's back. He wanted to move, but he couldn't. His legs wouldn't go.

"Where does the music come from? Gosh darnedest thing I ever saw," the voice went on.

Albert opened his mouth. Nothing came out.

"Can't you talk?" The radio floated back to the desk. "What are those ugly things?"

Albert's blue shirt swooped up from the floor and flung itself over his skull collection. It covered all the skulls except the cow's horns.

"Your eyes are poppin' out of your head," the voice said. "You ought to see yourself."

Albert's mouth moved at last. "How did you do that?" He stood up and took a step. A dog yelped.

Albert didn't have a dog.

He couldn't see a dog.

"You oughtn't to kick at Rags, he doesn't like being kicked at," the voice said.

Albert stared at the open closet door. The clothes were jiggling. Someone must be hiding there. Brian? He'd just left Brian on the corner.

Sally? His sister Sally was three years older than he was, but not smart enough to pull this. It couldn't be Sally.

"All right, I give up. Those were neat tricks. Now come out and show me how you did them," he said.

"Didn't do any tricks. Don't think I remember any tricks, tell the truth. You didn't tell me what the box was." The radio moved again.

Albert grabbed for it. "Cut it out! Just stop it. Where are you, anyhow?"

"Right here, of course."

"I can't see you."

"I know you can't. Wait a minute."

Albert heard someone breathing, and a pair of checkered knee pants appeared out of nowhere. Albert clutched the chair; the prickles were all over him now and he wished he could just run for it. He couldn't. His legs felt glued to the floor.

"Gosh-a-mighty—" said the voice, and then, all at once, a boy stood in the room, wearing the checkered pants and grinning. "I did it!" he cried. Albert, in one leap, landed by the door. "Hey, don't run away, I didn't mean to scare you."

Clutching the doorknob, Albert turned to look. Now the boy held a dog. A black and gray dog with tangled hair and two bright eyes peering out.

"What are you doing in my room? I don't even know you!"

"Come back then. I don't know as I can stay this way very long."

Albert stared at the boy and decided he was dreaming. No sense in being scared of a dream. He let the doorknob go, strolled across to the bed and sat on the lower bunk.

"Have a chair," he said. "Is that Rags?"

"Of course it is. What's your name?"

"Albert Shook."

The boy sat down, still holding the dog. "That's a good one. You're Albert Shook and you sure are shook up, right?"

Albert had heard that sort of joke before. He ignored it and asked the boy his name.

"Otis White, of course. They just pulled my house down, right down without any warning at all. One minute we were comfortable, the next minute—crash! You should have seen it, Albert. Rags and me just got out in time."

Albert reminded himself that it was only a dream. He knew Miss Dolly White's old house was gone. He'd watched the trucks carry away the last pieces after school. He knew that Otis was the name of Miss Dolly's brother, who got himself killed a long time ago.

"A horse landed on you," Albert said.

"I know that. I chased Rags out in front of Miller's ice wagon, and this horse was racing down the street— I never even saw him." Otis pulled his legs up and crossed them, dumping Rags off onto the floor. "My pa shot the horse," he said.

Albert pulled his legs up, too, and soberly studied Otis. Black and white checkered knee pants and black socks pulled up to meet them. Wide black suspenders over a white shirt. Blonde, straight hair that came down over his forehead, right to the top of the brightest blue eyes Albert had ever seen. And freckles, all over his face. One spot, below his left ear, was all brown, as though the freckles had run together.

"Got me memorized?" asked Otis. He slapped his knees. "This is something, this is. Only other time I tried it, Dolly saw me. Scared her something awful, I did."

"Where've you been since then?" asked Albert.

"I told you, in the house. Up in the attic in the little round room. Dolly locked us in there—said we'd worry Ma."

"I didn't know you could lock up a ghost."

"I don't know, never met any other ghosts. But we didn't have nowhere to go, anyhow."

Otis scooped Rags up into his arms and hugged him, then looked at Albert with a funny look on his face, almost a scared look.

"Listen," he said, "where is Dolly? Did she let them knock down our house?"

Albert thought this dream was getting difficult. He put his feet down and moved over a little, on the bed.

"She died last winter, Otis. But she was about eighty-five, you know. She was—"

"Eighty-five? Dolly was? Then—gosh, Albert, that means I'm eighty-seven. That's pretty funny, that is. That horse kicked me in nineteen aught three, you know. I was going to be twelve the next week."

"Miss Dolly always whispered when she talked about you," Albert said.

"Did she? Probably afraid I'd hear her. I never did, of course. I never heard nothing. You should have seen that house go down, Albert. My pa would have yelled, I'll tell you that. He'd have had ten fits. Never anything so exciting on our street before."

Albert was glad that Otis had changed the subject. "I was in school," he said.

"Monstrous big machines, just pushed it down and carried it away."

"They were bulldozers," Albert said. "And trucks." He felt dizzy. This had to be a dream!

"I sat out on the wall, part they didn't break down, and I didn't see one horse, Albert. Not one. Saw automobiles, at least I suppose they were automobiles. Didn't look like my pa's, though."

"Did they have cars in 1903?"

"Pa did. Mr. Harris did. There were four in town. Didn't look like the ones I saw today. I'd sure like to ride in one of those."

Albert closed his eyes. He squeezed them together. In dreams, if you wake up, it goes away, right? He opened his eyes and Otis was still there, still talking.

"People were wearing the funniest looking clothes, and why, there were three stores across the street, where the Johnsons live. Stores! Mrs. Johnson must be pretty upset about those stores, she was awful fussy about the neighborhood."

Albert was confused. There weren't any Johnsons across the street.

"Ice cream, the sign said. I like ice cream real well, but when I tried to cross the street, whammo! Couldn't do it. I can walk all around our yard, and I came in here all right, but not across the street." Otis scratched at his hair, looking puzzled. Then he nodded. "Of course, this is all Pa's land. I suppose that's why."

"This is our house," Albert said. "Not your pa's."

"Is it? It used to be our carriage house. I came in—"

"How? By the door?"

"Of course by the door. You let it slam right through me. Then you came up here and dropped your clothes on the floor, and sat down in this chair." Otis was quiet for a few moments; then he sighed. "What I'd like to know is how long does a person stay a ghost? Do you know that, Albert?"

"Of course I don't know that!" Albert started to laugh, and then didn't. Otis looked awfully serious. "How would I know that?"

"Well—" Otis looked down at the desk and Albert's paper. "Long division—I used to like long division. You don't get it though, do you? You have three problems wrong."

"I only did three problems."

"I know." Otis picked up the pencil.

Albert unfolded his legs and walked quietly to the door. He'd had enough of this dream.

"Listen, you don't eat, do you? I've got to set the table."

"I'd like to eat, but I guess I don't." Otis answered without looking up from the paper.

"Well, nice to meet you, Otis. See you around, okay?" He opened the door and stopped Rags with his foot. "Call your dog, will you? He'd just get into trouble downstairs."

"Rags!"

The little dog looked reproachfully at Albert, then

dashed across and settled on Otis's feet. Albert slid past the door, shut it, and took a deep breath. Then he ran.

Seconds later he landed in a heap at the bottom of the steps, two flights down in the living room. Some crazy dream that was, a ghost in his room.

Albert pinched himself, and it hurt. I'm awake now, he thought. Some crazy dream.

Chapter 2

Albert Wakes Up

Albert plopped four placemats onto the table and put the silverware around. He kept thinking about his dream. Otis White wasn't really up in his room, he thought. Otis couldn't be up in his room.

"What's taking you so long?" his mother said. "Get the milk and water, Albert, and call Dad and Sally. Wake up!"

He moved, then. But he kept thinking about it. He couldn't stop thinking about it. At the table, he ate as quickly as he could.

"You're getting spaghetti sauce all over your shirt, Albert," his mother told him.

"That's normal," Sally said. "Did you see Miss Dolly's house tonight? Isn't it awful, what they did?"

"Nothing left to see," Mr. Shook said. "It doesn't

15

take long these days, once they start to demolish a house."

Mrs. Shook told Albert to eat his salad. "Having a brand new library next door will be wonderful," she added.

"Yeah, I'll get to use the new computer anytime I want," Albert said. "I can sign up first thing. They have these games—"

"Games!" Sally said. "That's so dumb, Albert. What about the movies? They're going to have this series— Great Monster Movies!"

"Computers are not dumb. They have these programs on cassettes, you know, and—"

His mother interrupted. "I was thinking of your schoolwork," she said. "You'll be able to use the whole library for your research projects."

"That's not worth tearing down a house for." Albert decided that as long as they were talking about the house he could ask a dumb-sounding question. "What happens to the ghosts, when they tear down an old house like that?"

"Never thought about it," said his father. "But I doubt there were any ghosts in that place. Miss Dolly would have moved them or herself, long ago."

"But what if they were family ghosts?" Albert looked earnestly at his father. He usually answered Albert's questions carefully, and he didn't often laugh at him. But this time he might.

"Dolly was afraid of the least little thing," Mrs. Shook

said. "But there are no such things as ghosts, Albert. Don't worry."

"I'm not worrying." From where he sat, Albert could see his mother's bell collection on the living room window sill. A pink china bell moved into the air and turned upside down.

"What was that?"

"What?" asked Albert.

"That tinkling sound." His mother pushed her chair back. "Is someone—"

"Just the ice cream truck," Albert said, thinking fast.

His mother sat back. He watched, horrified, while the pink bell moved back in place without a sound. The weird prickles danced again, up his back and into his hair.

Albert thought that a dream which followed him down to dinner was a pretty strange dream. "About those ghosts," he said. "I just wondered where they would go, if there were any, I mean."

"They wouldn't go far," said his father. "Ghosts usually stay where they lived before, as I understand it."

"John—" Mrs. Shook looked disgusted. "There are no ghosts."

"I know. But if there were any, I suppose they would move into the new library. The White Memorial Library, according to Miss Dolly's will. It's logical that a White ghost should live in the White Library." He passed the spaghetti bowl to Albert. "Eat up, you'll need your strength. It's our night to do the dishes, remember."

They took turns by the week, Albert drying the dishes his father washed, one week, Sally and their mother doing it the next.

As they finished the dishes this night, Mr. Shook mentioned the ghosts again.

"You aren't really worried? You haven't met any, have you?" Mr. Shook never blinked at any possibility. Albert almost told him about Otis. Then he reminded himself it was just a dream. He must have dreamed that bell moving around, too.

"No. Anyhow, I don't think I have," he said.

His father stopped wiping the table to look thoughtfully at Albert. "No? Well, if you do, don't introduce them to your mother. She would not care to meet one socially."

Albert grinned. "She said there were no such things as ghosts, remember?"

"Certainly. She doesn't believe in anything she cannot see or touch."

Albert thought about that while he hung his dish towel to dry.

"She believes in love, doesn't she? You can't see or touch that."

"Albert, you are becoming a philosopher. Love is real to your mother, I agree. Ghosts are not." Mr. Shook started for the living room and the evening paper. "Homework?"

"Finished three problems. I'll get back to it. I promised to meet Brian first, though." He let the screen door slam behind him and raced across the back yard. Their tree house, which was more of a platform with sides, was fitted around a thick branch of the maple tree behind the garage. Once up, you could look down on the garage roof or the garden, over the lawn toward Carrie Snyder's house and their swimming pool, or the other way where Miss Dolly's house used to be. By fall, they would look down on the parking lot of the new library.

Brian was already there, looking over the railing, when Albert heaved himself up through the hole and sprawled onto the platform. "Sure looks funny at Miss Dolly's place, doesn't it?" he said. "Boards and bricks and glass all over, and a bulldozer sitting in her garden."

"Yeah." Albert rested his elbows on the railing, too, and they contemplated the strange scene.

"Remember how Miss Dolly paid us nickels to keep the twigs off the sidewalk?" Brian shook his head. "She'd hate that mess."

"But the library was her own idea, remember," Albert said. "I hope they don't take down all the trees."

"At least they won't take down this one. It's in your yard."

"What do you think about—" Albert stopped. He wasn't sure he wanted to ask.

"What do I think about what?"

"Well—about ghosts. What do you think happens to the ghosts when an old house like that gets torn down? What do you think?"

Brian's shiny, round face looked surprised. He sat back on his heels and looked at Albert.

"I think you are nuts," he said. "Miss Dolly wouldn't come around as a ghost."

"I know that. But there might be others. You know, from way back. What would they do?"

"You're sick." Brian said. "There aren't any ghosts, and you know it. Except in castles, maybe. Boy, you are dumb."

He opened the box where they kept things safe from the rain and stuffed a comic book inside. "I've got to go home, I said I'd be back before dark."

"Me, too. I have a whole page of long division to do. Look, Brian. See that branch wiggling over the yard?" Albert pointed toward Miss Dolly's rose bushes, near the side of the drive. "That could be a ghost pulling it. A ghost dog, maybe."

Brian looked at the branch. It moved jerkily across an open space.

"The wind," he said, and let his feet down through the hole. "Forget about ghosts and figure out how we can fix this ladder. We've got to fix the ladder."

"You just have to stop eating so much is all," Albert said. He watched Brian let himself down the rope ladder, then put his feet through. "If you didn't eat so much, you could do this—" and he caught a lower branch and went hand over hand until it let him down, within jumping distance. He jumped.

Brian said he could do that, he just hadn't thought of it. They parted by the back door of Albert's house.

Albert thought he would watch a television show, but his mother said he'd better finish his math.

He thought he would have a little snack, but his mother said he had just finished supper. "Do your homework, Albert. Up," she said, pointing at the stairway. He went up.

He paused at the door of his old room on the second floor. When he moved to the attic a month ago, his mother moved her office in here. She was the editor of a little magazine, and needed room to spread out, she said. Albert grinned. She sure had spread out, all over the place. She was always complaining about his messy room, but these piles of books and papers were just as bad. Of course, she would say these were important.

Albert thought his things were important, too.

Albert went up the next flight and slowly opened the door. He reached in and flicked on the light. He looked inside. No one here. Empty. He sighed with relief. It was just a dream, he thought. A crazy dream, because Miss Dolly had told him about Otis so many times.

Albert tossed his red jacket in the general direction of the closet door. He sat down at the desk and picked up the pencil. He looked at the paper—and swallowed, hard.

The problems were done. Not just the first three, but the whole page. Twenty long division, finished.

Chapter Three

You Wouldn't Believe!

Before Albert went to school the next day, his mother made a speech. He had heard it before.

"Today, this very day, Albert, you are to clean up your room. Pick up your clothes, straighten everything up, and throw out half that junk. You cannot live in that mess, Albert!"

"But I like it that way. I know where everything is," he said.

"This very afternoon, Albert. You must begin to show some sense of responsibility."

Albert did not want a sense of responsibility. It was bad enough to have a ghost, he thought, but he did not tell his mother that. Besides, maybe Otis would never come back. He hadn't been around last night, at all. At least, he hadn't talked, or shown himself.

Albert yawned. He had stayed awake a long time

last night. It was hard to go to sleep when a ghost dog might land on you, or a ghost boy ask a question. Now he was sleepy, and he had to go to school.

When he came home at three-thirty, his mother was waiting in the kitchen.

"Albert—"

"I will. I'm going right up, honest."

"No jokes, Albert." Her eyes smiled at him, while she tried to look cross. "Why did you let me lecture you this morning, when your room was already neat as a pin?"

Albert's mouth dropped open. He shut it. He put his arithmetic book on the table and said slowly, "Did I do that?"

"You know you did. I'm so proud of you, dear. I do believe you are developing that sense of responsibility." She kissed him and pointed to the cookies cooling on the table. "You did forget to turn off the radio, however. I heard music when I went up to my office. That's why I went to your room. You really must remember to turn things off if you want to sleep in the attic, Albert."

Albert remembered clearly that he had turned the radio off.

"I think I'll go outside," he said.

"Not in those clothes. Go upstairs and change first."

Albert was not anxious to go upstairs, but he could see there was no use arguing about it. His mother would win.

She picked up his book. "Homework? Maybe you'd better—"

"Got every single problem right, today," he told her. "Every single one."

"That's wonderful. Now, go and change, dear. I have work to do before suppertime."

He listened as she went up to her office, then followed her slowly. He wasn't afraid of Otis, exactly. But he wasn't used to ghosts. Especially ghosts who cleaned your room. It wasn't very ghost-like, Albert thought.

He pulled the door shut at the bottom of the attic steps, took a deep breath, and went up. At the top there were two doors, his own and one to a storage area on the right. He opened his door.

"Thought you'd never get here," Otis said.

Albert looked around. The room was cold, but it was neat. Come to think of it, it had been cold last night, too. He stepped inside and saw that the bed was made and the skulls covered up again. He couldn't see Otis.

"So where are you?"

"Up here, of course."

Albert looked up at the top bunk and Otis appeared; all at once, this time.

"I'm getting better," he said, in a pleased voice. "It isn't so hard to materialize, once you get the hang of it." He snapped his fingers. "Come on, Rags, you can do it—" and the little dog was suddenly there. He barked at Albert.

"Hey! Make him stop that. My Mom will be up here looking for a dog."

"Turn the knob on the black box, then. She'll think it is coming out of that."

"Radio," Albert said. "It's a radio."

"Where does the music come from? I turned the knob today and the sound came out. Your mother turned it off again."

"I know. You can't go turning knobs, Otis. And besides that, you shouldn't have messed up my room like this." He shivered. "It's cold up here."

"Your mother said you had to clean it up. I heard her. Me and Rags didn't have anything else to do. I figured you'd be glad."

"Well, I guess I am." Albert dropped onto the chair and grinned at Otis. "All the same, if she'd come up here and seen the mess this morning, and then found it all cleaned up this afternoon, when I was at school the whole time—" Albert laughed. "How could I explain that? She doesn't believe in ghosts."

"I never did, either. I don't think you know where the music comes from," Otis said. He dropped to the floor and picked up the radio.

"I do, too. It comes through the air."

"Huh. Show me."

Albert tossed his shirt toward the clothes basket in the corner and pulled an orange sweatshirt over his head. He dropped his school pants and pulled on his old jeans.

"Wait right here," he said.

He raced downstairs and came back with a World Book in his hand. He saw that his pants were hung from a hook on the door, and his shirt was actually in the basket.

"If my mother believed in you, she'd like you," he said. "Here, you can read all about it, yourself."

Both boys bent over the book. Otis read out loud. ". . . 'changes sound waves to radio waves.' Yes, but it doesn't say how."

Albert turned the page. "Here it does." He waited for Otis to read it. "See, I was right. Through the air," he said. He cautiously pulled the blue shirt from his skull collection while Otis read it again. If radio was a surprise, Albert thought, what about television? And a lot of other things. If Otis expected him to explain all the inventions since 1903, he was in trouble. He'd better move the whole set of World Books up here.

The telephone rang in his parents' bedroom, downstairs. Rags barked and Otis straightened up.

"What is that? I heard it a lot today."

"The telephone, of course."

"Oh. Doesn't sound like our telephone. My pa said he wouldn't have one in the house, long as Jean Conners was the operator. She listened to everyone talking. Ma said we had to have one, so we did, but Pa was right."

"Did she really listen to you talking?"

"Sure she did. One time Pud and me planned this good trick on Mr. Smithers, our teacher. But we planned it on the telephone and that was pretty dumb."

Albert sat down on the bottom bunk and crossed his legs. "What kind of trick?" he asked.

"Frogs. We caught ourselves two jars of spring peepers. Pud figured we could hide them in the cloakroom and they would drive teacher clear out of his mind with their noise. He'd think they were outdoors, you see."

"Did you do it?" Albert couldn't imagine doing something like that at his school.

"Well, course we did. But old operator Jean listened in and told teacher, and the day we sneaked them into the room, real early, and they were peeping away, Mr. Smithers taught a whole long lesson on tree frogs, first thing in the morning, and he made us go and get them to show everyone, just as though he'd planned it that way. Then he gave us a test on the whole thing. And then—" Otis sat down on the floor and began to tease Rags. Finally he looked back at Albert, and went on, "then he made us go out in the schoolyard, down by the creek, and let all those peepers go free again. Some trick that turned out to be."

Albert grinned. "It could have been worse, I guess."

"Sure, he could have used his paddle on us again. Pud wore cardboard in his pants all through the fifth grade. Said it pays to be prepared."

Albert wished he'd known Pud.

"Anyhow, it was a good trick, if only that operator had minded her own business. Does your operator listen in?"

"We don't have operators except for finding numbers and making long distance calls, and sometimes not even then," Albert said. He didn't think he could explain direct dialing to Otis this afternoon, or any afternoon, come to that. "Listen, we have to talk about what to do with you," he said.

"Don't need to be done to. I like it here. Didn't have a radio in my attic. Didn't have anything up there."

"What did you do all the time?"

Otis looked puzzled. "Well, when Dolly locked us in, I knew that didn't matter. I'd gone right through walls already, you see. But she said I would upset Ma, and I didn't want to upset anybody. Especially Ma. We didn't know what else to do, so we just stayed there—sort of hovering, I guess you'd call it. Like sleeping."

"For seventy-five years? Even Rip Van Winkle didn't sleep that long."

"Yes, but he wasn't a ghost, you know. We'd probably be sleeping now, if they hadn't knocked our house down. We were comfortable, weren't we, Rags?"

The little dog barked and Albert looked nervously toward the door.

"He's got to stop barking like that."

"He'll learn. Honest, he will." Otis looked out the window, then back at Albert. "I'm glad they knocked us out of our attic, Albert. I like it here fine. You don't have to do nothing about us."

"Where'd you go, last night?"

"To sleep, of course."

Albert looked around, then back at Otis. "Where?"

"In that funny bed on top of yours. It was nice."

Albert sank down on his bed and poked at the springs

of the upper bunk. Right there, he thought. He shivered. Ghosts sleeping right there over my head all night long. He sat up again. Now he was the one looking puzzled.

"You know that doesn't make sense? I mean, ghosts are supposed to walk around at night. How come you sleep at night and go around cleaning up folk's rooms in the daytime?"

"Rags doesn't like the dark, that's why."

Albert stared at Otis, then fell back on the bed, laughing. "A ghost dog afraid of the dark!—Hey!" Rags had jumped on top of him, and was tugging at his shirt. "Cut that out!"

"Stop it, Rags. I—whoops!" Otis disappeared. Rags jumped toward the floor, but before he landed he too disappeared. "Can't stay that way long at a time yet," Otis said. "But I'll get better with a little practice."

Albert said he was going and slipped out the door. He raced down and out of the house, through the hedge and into Carrie's yard, next door. She sat under the sycamore tree, building something, as usual. She was going to be an engineer someday.

"Who's chasing you? You look all funny, Albert."

"I feel sort of funny." He flopped down on the grass and let out a long sigh. Otis couldn't come over here. This had never been White property. He watched Carrie for a moment. She was making a bridge of stones across a gully in the sycamore roots.

One stone looked loose to Albert. He put a hand out

to steady it and that end of the bridge fell with a rattle and a plop.

"Oh, Albert—" Carrie pushed his hand away. "Don't help, okay? I'm the engineer, not you."

"Some engineer. I only touched it and it fell down."

"That's because it isn't finished. This end holds up that end, you see?" Carrie patiently put stone on stone, building it again. "No wonder your Dad won't get you a new bike. He probably thinks you'd wreck it, first thing."

Albert grunted. He looked toward the garage, where the tail of his green bike stuck out. It wasn't just old, it was ancient. His father had used it in college. It was made before hand brakes had been invented, he thought. Going up hills on that old bike was a pain. Especially when everyone else had gears, and just sailed up and away.

"Don't look so gloomy, you'll get a new one," Carrie said. "Someday," she added.

"Yeah, when I've developed a sense of responsibility. My gosh, Carrie, you'd think I didn't even try."

"Well, breaking those garage windows wouldn't be so bad if you'd fix them, Albert. It's been a month."

"Glass is expensive," he said.

"And that F in Social Studies last six weeks didn't help," Carrie said. "Just because you didn't do your notebook."

"I hate notebooks!"

"But you have a good stamp album, and you like it."

"That's not homework," Albert said. "That's different."

Carrie said that was not reasonable, and Albert opened his mouth to argue when he heard his mother yell.

"Albert!"

"Sounds like she's seen a ghost," Carrie said.

Albert scrambled to his feet. He'd forgotten Otis. How could he forget Otis?

His mother stood on the back steps, her hands on her hips. "Why did you turn on every radio in the house?"

"I did? Every one?"

"Don't quibble, Albert. If you missed one, I don't know where. What possessed you? The noise is frightful."

"But Mom, I—" Albert stopped. If he said he hadn't done it, how could he explain? He shut his mouth.

"Go turn them off and stay in your room until suppertime." She turned back, into the house. "There can't be a reasonable explanation," she said.

Albert looked back at Carrie and shrugged his shoulders, helplessly.

"But why did you do it, Albert?" she asked.

"If I explained, you'd never believe me." He looked up toward his attic window, and shook his head. "Never," he said.

Chapter 4

Nothing Scares Carrie

Once you got used to it, it was interesting, having a ghost around. Especially a ghost who had been up in an attic room for seventy-five years, and didn't know anything about the modern world. Otis was amazed at everything from Albert's ballpoint pen to his digital alarm clock.

Otis was good at math. Every night he helped Albert with his problems, and Mrs. Murphy, Albert's teacher, was beginning to praise him for his good work. She even wrote a note to his parents, and they told Albert they were glad he was developing a sense of responsibility toward his homework, too.

His room stayed neat, because Otis couldn't abide a mess. That's what he said, and it must have been true. He hung Albert's clothes up every day, and kept the papers and books in neat piles, no matter how Albert scattered them.

"It doesn't feel comfortable," Albert muttered. "Doesn't feel right." But Otis picked things up anyhow, and covered the skull collection every day. He didn't like skulls.

Otis didn't understand social studies, though. He didn't even know what that meant. When Albert explained, Otis said that was geography, or history. He didn't see why they were lumped together.

"Right now we're studying the United States," Albert told him one evening. "I have to write a report on Alaska before next Friday."

"Alaska? That's not a united state."

Albert gave a disgusted snort. "I'll prove it." He ran downstairs and was back in a minute with the "A" volume of the *World Book*. "I wish I *had* brought the whole set up here." He looked around for Otis. "You'd be easier to talk to if I could see you," he said.

"I'm tired."

"Then go to sleep and let me finish my homework." He turned the pages quickly. "Here it is. Alaska is the forty-ninth state. Became a state in 1959."

"Forty-ninth? But—" There was a long pause. "Got it. Utah was the forty-fifth state, I remember I got that right on a test."

"There's a lot happened since that horse got you."

"Read it to me," Otis said.

Albert read the sections about Alaska becoming a state. When he finished he flipped over a few pages and came to the entry on Astronauts. "Hey, Otis!" he said. "You don't know about space ships, do you?" Otis looked at him blankly. "You know, we've had men flying to the moon and walking around on it," Albert went on.

"You haven't either—how could you do that?"

"It's the truth," Albert said. He started to read the section on Astronauts. He got so interested he didn't hear his mother coming up the steps.

"Albert?" A quick knock and she stuck her head in. "You ought to be in bed. Are you reading to yourself?"

He stared at her. "It sticks in my mind better if I read it out loud," he said.

"Oh? Well, finish up and go to bed, dear."

When she was gone, Albert looked toward the top bunk. "You see? You'll get me in awful trouble yet."

But the next day he got an A in a social studies test, and hurried home to tell Otis about it.

"You're lucky to have me around," Otis said. "You wouldn't study hard enough without me."

Albert looked for his jeans and found them hanging on a hook. Otis was so neat it was disgusting. "Let's go and watch the library go up," he suggested.

"That's all I've done all day long. I've got a better idea." Otis materialized suddenly. He stretched and snapped his suspenders. "Let's go through the house. You promised we could someday, if I stayed up here. No one is home now, but us. I heard your ma go away a little while ago."

"I know. She left a note. But—"

"You promised."

"Okay, but no fooling around. I'll show you things, but you leave them alone."

They went together down the steps, and Albert showed Otis all around the house. Otis didn't leave things alone, but Albert guessed he wouldn't either, if he were Otis.

Otis turned lights on and off, played with the electric typewriter in Mrs. Shook's office, flushed the toilet six times and pretended to shave with Mr. Shook's electric razor. When Albert explained the washer and dryer in the basement, he said his Ma would sure have liked those things. "She always sneezed, hanging clothes out in the sunshine," he said.

His favorite thing was the record player. When Albert showed him the television, he was frightened, and made Albert turn it off again, but he loved the record player.

"Where's the crank?" he asked, first thing. "How do you wind it up?"

"You don't wind it, you plug it in. The electricity makes it run, see?" He pulled the plug and gave it to Otis.

"Everything in this house has a plug," Otis said. He pushed it into the wall socket. "My pa always said electricity could do more'n turn on lights."

"Now you push the lever," Albert told him. "The record plops down, the arm comes over and—there. It plays the music."

"Like magic," Otis said. "Pud's folks had a Gramophone you wind up and it'd go just fine until about the end of the record, and then the music slowed down and you had to hurry and crank it up again."

He watched the record going round and round.

"Show me again," he said.

Albert stopped the music and put another record on, something of Sally's with a disco beat. Otis pushed the lever, and sighed happily as the disc fell, the arm moved, and the music began.

"I call that some apples," he said.

Albert guessed it was, at that. He'd never thought about electricity being special before.

"You'll like the television when you get used to it," he told Otis. "Let's go watch the builders now."

"I'd rather stay and play records," Otis said. "I like that music, makes you feel like dancing." Albert shook his head.

"Sally will be home any minute," he said. "You'd better disappear. You can't go outdoors like that."

Otis disappeared.

"If Brian's out there, don't talk," Albert added. "We've got to figure out a way to introduce you without scaring him. And I haven't figured it out yet."

"How about Carrie? She doesn't look as though she'd be scared."

"She's a girl, isn't she? She'd be scared."

"I'm not so sure," Otis said.

Outdoors, Albert crawled up through the hole and onto the tree house platform. Otis came up, too, but how he did it, Albert couldn't see. Otis didn't know, either.

"I just kind of float," he always said, when Albert asked how he got places.

This afternoon, no one else was in the tree house, so Otis snapped his fingers and appeared. He always snapped his fingers now, just before he materialized.

"I wish you wouldn't do that. Some kid snapped his fingers in school today and scared me out of my wits," Albert said.

Otis laughed. "You know I can't go off White property," he said. Albert said he knew it, but he didn't believe everything he knew, anymore.

They sat in comfortable silence for awhile, watching as a crane lifted a steel beam.

"Look at that—" Otis sighed his relief as the beam settled into position. "That's something, that is." He slid down and pulled Rags into his arms. "Albert, when I'm not a ghost anymore, where do you suppose I'll go?"

"What in the world do you mean?" Albert turned to stare at Otis.

"I dunno. I don't see how to account for my being around all this time."

"Well—" Albert pulled a packet of chewing gum from his pocket and took one stick out. He rolled it up, put it in his mouth, and bit down slowly. He wanted to taste all the juice, and he wanted time to think.

"I want to be around," Otis said. "I like it here fine, you see."

Albert's eyes brightened; he pushed the gum back into the corner of his mouth. "Listen, that's probably the reason, you see? You want to be around, so you are. I bet you got to stop wanting, to stop being a ghost, you see, Otis?"

"But Dolly isn't a ghost. Pa isn't, or—"

"Yes, but Miss Dolly was old, Otis. She didn't want to be a ghost, I'll bet. And—" Rags barked, Albert shut his mouth, and both ghosts disappeared as Carrie's head came through the hole and she heaved herself up.

"I heard you, Albert Shook." She looked around, then scrambled to her feet. "You were doing it again, talking to yourself! Something is going on that I don't understand, Albert. Ever since that day you turned the radios on. Something funny is going on, and it's time you told me about it."

She sat down, folded her arms, and waited. Albert got up on his knees and looked over at the new building. "Library looks like a skeleton," he said. "It's going to be all done by the time school starts next year."

"You are not telling me, Albert." Carrie ran her fingers through her short hair, making it all stand on end. Albert grinned. One of these days, he supposed, she would be like Sally, fussing about how she looks. He was glad she hadn't started that yet.

"You're stubborn," he said.

"Well, what's going on? Brian said you must be mad

at him, or something. You never play after school anymore."

"Mrs. Murphy gives too much homework, that's all."

"That's a lie, Albert Shook. I'm in your class and I
don't have that much homework. You can fool Brian
with that, maybe, but not me."

"Well, I'm not mad at anyone. Just been busy."

"Doing what?"

Albert thought about saying he was busy finding out
how things work, but he knew what Carrie would say.
She would say he ought to ask her, because she already
knows how everything works. Which was true, but all
the same—

"Tell her, Albert," Otis said, and Carrie jumped to
her feet.

"Who said that?"

"No one said anything," Albert said, but Carrie
swung her arms around, and Otis gave a startled yell.
Rags barked. "For gosh sakes, Carrie, sit down!" yelled
Albert.

"I'm not sure I want to sit down." Carrie grabbed
the tree branch.

"Do it anyhow. You can't go around swinging at people."

"I didn't."

"You did!" Albert glared at her. "Go on home if you
are going to swing around hitting people."

"Albert, you are clear across there, I didn't hit you
and you know it."

"You hit me, is what you hit." Otis snapped his fingers and materialized. "At least, you would have hit me if there was anything of me to hit," he added, just as Brian's face appeared in the hole.

"What are you all yelling about?" he asked, and then he saw Otis. His mouth dropped open. Rags appeared, in Otis's arms, and Brian gave a yell, dropped out of the hole and fell on the ground. Seconds later he disappeared around the garage.

Carrie sat down and grinned at Otis. "You sure scared him," she said.

Albert yelled at Brian to come back. Then he turned and shrugged his shoulders. "I told you," he began, then sank back on the floor, laughing. "You were right, Otis. Nothing can scare Carrie."

"Am I supposed to be scared? I figured if you weren't, I didn't need to be."

"You see?" Otis sat down, settled Rags on his knees, and told Carrie that he was Otis White.

"You are?" She frowned, and then her eyes lit with delight and she laughed. "Miss Dolly's brother! A real, live ghost," she said.

"That's the dumbest thing I ever heard," Albert told her, "but you are right. He is a ghost, and what I'm supposed to do with him I do not know."

"I keep telling you, I don't need doing with. Carrie, do you know how long a person stays a ghost?"

Carrie looked thoughtful, then said she didn't. "Until just now, Otis, I didn't know there really was such a thing as a ghost. So how could I know that?"

"That's right." Otis looked sad a second longer. Then

his bright eyes turned brighter and he leaned toward Carrie. "But you do know about cars, don't you? You're going to be an engineer, someday, aren't you? Do you know how a car works?"

"Of course I do," Carrie said. "But I'm not allowed to drive until I'm sixteen. That's five more years."

"But can you show me? I'm old enough. I'm eighty-seven. At least I would be, if I weren't a ghost."

"That's old enough," Carrie grinned. "Come on, I'll show you." She put her feet through the hole, caught the ladder and went down to the ground. Otis disappeared, and a moment later Albert heard him explaining that he figured it would be better if no one saw him.

"Well, that makes sense," Carrie said. "Come on."

Albert pulled his legs up and settled his chin in his knees. If Otis learns to drive a car, that will be trouble. No good can come of this, he thought. No good at all.

Chapter 5

Missing Teeth

Albert felt responsible for Otis and Rags, even though he knew he wasn't. He waited in the tree house for a while, but when Carrie and Otis didn't come back he went hand over hand down the branch, and dropped to the ground. He felt responsible for Brian, too, even if it wasn't his fault that Otis and Rags appeared and scared him. He had to find him.

Albert inched his way along the side of the house away from the garage, out to the front yard. Then he raced across the street, and stopped. He looked back. He'd heard a bark, but he couldn't see Rags. Anyhow, neither Rags nor Otis could follow him here. It never had been White property on this side of the street.

He found Brian sitting on the steps of his apartment house, staring into space. His shiny, round face still looked surprised.

43

"Why did you run?" Albert asked, settling down beside him. Brian moved away a bit. "You didn't need to run like that."

"Oh yes I did," Brian said. He opened his fingers in the air and looked at them. "There wasn't anyone in the tree house," he said. "Then you went up, all alone. Then Carrie went up. Then—"

"How do you know there wasn't anyone there?"

"Because I was spying. I was hiding back of the garage, going to surprise you, but I heard you yelling, and Carrie yelling, and—" Brian took a deep breath. "Then I went up and that kid was there, with knee pants on, and a dog that wasn't there and then was there." He stopped. "I didn't see that really, did I?"

"Sure you did. That's Otis and Rags."

Brian's face turned as white as his t-shirt.

"You don't need to be scared of them. That's Otis White, Miss Dolly's brother, the one that got killed when she was a little girl. And Rags is his dog."

Brian stared at his fingers. He bent each one down, then straightened them out. He stood up.

"There's no such thing as ghosts," he said, backing up toward the door.

"There are," Albert said. "When they knocked down Miss Dolly's house, Otis and Rags didn't have an attic room anymore. They moved into my room. They've been there for weeks now. I tried to tell you the first day, but when I mentioned ghosts, you said you had to go home."

"No such things as ghosts," Brian said, his hand on the door knob.

"Listen, they can't come over here, they can't go off the old White property. Sit down and let me tell you."

Brian shouted, "No such things as ghosts!" He opened the door and raced up the steps.

For the next two weeks, until school was out for the summer, Brian didn't speak to Albert. Albert was too busy to worry about that. Carrie came over every day to explain things to Otis. Albert tried to look as though Carrie were talking to him, in case anyone saw them. It made him so nervous he hardly heard a word.

One afternoon Mrs. Shook came in with her arms filled with books. She went upstairs to her office, but seconds later was back in the kitchen, her hands on her hips, staring at Albert and Sally.

"My office, which one of you went into my office?"

Albert couldn't say a word. He didn't dare. Sally looked confused. "What's wrong with your office?" she asked.

"It's neat, that's what is wrong. My books and all the papers in neat piles. I don't need any help up there, thank you. Those things were organized exactly as I wanted them." She stopped talking and just stared at Albert. Then she said, "Albert, are you responsible for this?"

Albert thought fast. "Responsible?" he said. "You keep telling me to be responsible, and neat, and I thought—"

She sighed. "Albert, I know you meant well, dear, but—" she smiled and explained that sometimes she needed to spread out. "To see the whole picture," she said.

Albert hurried upstairs to find Otis.

"But I was trying to help," Otis said, as soon as Albert stopped yelling at him. "That room was a mess, and I can't abide a mess. You kn⌐⌐ that."

"Otis, I've got to do somet⌐⌐ bout you," Albert said, for the hundredth time.

"But I like it here." Otis's freckled face grew sober and he looked worried. "Besides, I don't know what would happen to me if I stopped being a ghost, Albert. Please don't do nothing about me."

A few days later Mrs. Shook raised Albert's allowance by fifty cents a week.

"Because I do appreciate your room, Albert. It is always neat. You are truly growing more responsible."

He kept the money. He couldn't explain to his mother that he hadn't earned it, that Otis was the neat one.

One night Mr. Shook came up to Albert's attic, to see for himself. "Good heavens! Is this really your room, Albert? Are you ill?" He sat down on the desk chair and looked around in mock despair. "How can you find anything?" Then he shivered. "Cold up here," he said. "That's strange. Feels like March instead of May."

Albert said it must be the insulation they put in, but he knew it wasn't. It was always cold when Otis was near. Even Rags left a trail of cold air when he ran through a place. Albert had decided that cold air and his ghosts went together.

"Now that I think of it, it's been a bit cold downstairs, too, and that is strange, this time of year." Mr. Shook looked seriously at Albert. "When Sally and I played Scrabble on Sunday afternoon, it was so cold by my chair I put a sweater on."

"That's funny," Albert said. He wondered what his father would say if he told him that Otis had watched the game. Actually, his father was lucky Otis hadn't started making words for him. Otis liked Scrabble. He also liked checkers and rummy.

Mr. Shook went downstairs, but before he left the room he stood looking at Albert again. "Interesting. Your room has been neat for weeks, your mother tells me. You are always on time for meals, you no longer race off with Brian, bicycle flags waving. You spend most of the time here or sitting in the tree house. Sure you don't have a problem I can help with?"

Albert tried to look cheerful. "No, I'm fine, really. Up in the tree house we can watch them building the library. Did you see how fast they got that frame up—"

"I know. Now the slow part. But Albert, I can see Carrie spending her time watching a building grow, but you? Not your thing, I'd have thought."

Mr. Shook went downstairs, and Albert wondered if Otis had heard all that. He asked, but Otis didn't answer. He was probably in the garage, pretending to drive Mom's car. Albert worried a lot about that.

The Sunday after school was out, Albert forgot to worry about the car. He and his dad were planting beans in the garden, his mother was supervising, when Sally ran screaming out of the house.

"My teeth! My teeth are gone! I can't find them anywhere!" She fell in a heap on the grass.

"Did you look in a glass by your bed?" asked Albert. Miss Dolly used to put hers in a glass; he thought that was neat.

Sally made a horrible face at him, all her braces shining in the sunlight.

"Just don't be funny, Albert. You know what I mean."

Albert did know what she meant. When she first went to that special dentist, the orthodontist, he made a plaster cast of her teeth. She wasn't supposed to take it away from his office until her teeth were all straightened, until the braces came off. But she did.

"Why did you bring them home?" asked Mr. Shook.

"To show Elizabeth. She wouldn't believe me when I said they looked so gross, so Dr. Miles said I could." Sally gave a great, shuddering sigh. "He will murder me if I don't bring them back tomorrow, and now they're gone. I can't find them anyplace."

"They couldn't be gone," Mother said. "They were on the shelf in the bookcase. Now just stop and think, Sally. Where might you have put them?"

"I didn't. I didn't move them at all." Sally's face

crumpled, ready to cry. Albert opened his mouth and she added, "Just shut up, Albert. Unless you tell me where you put them."

"Albert?" His father's left eyebrow went up.

"I didn't. I swear. I wouldn't touch those things. My gosh, Dad, have you really looked at them? Ugh!"

Mother and Sally went into the house. Albert sat back on his heels and thought about Otis, then shook his head. No, Otis wouldn't bother Sally's plaster teeth. Otis liked mechanical things, not teeth that just sit.

Albert rolled his tongue over his own teeth and was glad they were coming in straight. He didn't want braces if he could help it. Or white plaster teeth, either.

Soon Mrs. Shook called them and the search for the plaster teeth began in earnest. They turned everything upside down, from the front door to the back. No teeth.

"Someone has stolen them," Sally declared, and Albert laughed.

"Who would steal an ugly mold of your teeth?"

"Well, they're gone," she said. "Someone did."

"If we had a dog," Albert said, "he would find them for you."

"We don't have a dog. Anyhow, a dog would probably chew them up." Tears rolled down Sally's face. Albert decided to find Otis—and Rags.

He went to the tree house. No Otis. He checked in the garage, walked down the sidewalk around Miss Dolly's lot, out to the main street and checked the little bit of wall where Otis liked to sit.

He wasn't there. At least, Albert couldn't see him.

He sat down and called, but no one answered. He whistled, but Rags didn't bark.

Finally, he went up to his attic room. No Otis. The radio was on though, so maybe he had just missed him.

After supper, made miserable by Sally's unhappy face and occasional sobs, Albert went to the tree house and waited. Otis appeared just before dark.

"I been waiting for you upstairs," he said.

"I've been looking for you everywhere," Albert said. "Where have you been all day?"

"Here and there. Carrie and me—" Otis stopped and started over. "Carrie and I watched the builders for awhile. Going to be a big library, you know? A lot of folks come to watch. They sit on that wall. Old Rags got sat on a couple of times and was he mad! Didn't bark, though." Otis grabbed Rags and ruffled his fur. "He went off by himself and I had to hunt for him. Silly old dog."

"Where did you find him?"

"Up in your room. Come on, let's go."

Otis sounded excited. Albert couldn't see a thing to be excited about. He climbed down out of the tree-house and they went into the house. Upstairs, they played rummy, and Otis kept looking up as if he were waiting for something. At last Albert said he was going to bed. He went to the bathroom, called goodnight to his family downstairs, came back and climbed into bed. Then he remembered he hadn't asked Otis about the teeth, and he looked up.

"Ye-ow!" Albert let out a yell before he could stop it.

"Thought you'd never look," Otis said. "Do you like them?"

"Like them! Where did you get those things?" Albert rushed across the room, yanked his blue shirt from the skull collection and uncovered the plaster teeth, sitting right on the edge. Albert grabbed them. "Where did you find these?"

"Rags did. Aren't they awful? I figured you'd like them for your dumb collection. Thought when you took the cover off, the way you always do, you'd see them. But tonight you didn't take it off."

"I saw the end just now, when I looked at you. Otis, we looked for those things everywhere, today. Rags—where's Rags?"

"Under the blanket."

"He'd better stay there. Did he carry them upstairs?"

"No, he came rolling them out when I went in once to listen to Sally play a record. I brought them upstairs."

"Oh, boy." Albert sat down, overcome by the vision of the plaster mold floating through the air, up the stairs—what if Sally had seen them? "Now the problem is what to do with them!"

"Don't you want them for the collection?"

"Of course not." He explained to Otis about the orthodontist.

"So that's what she has on her teeth! I couldn't figure it out," Otis said. "I wanted to ask, but I didn't like to hurt your feelings."

"Didn't anyone wear braces in 1903?"

"If they did, I never saw them. Some folks could have used them, though."

Albert flopped onto the bed. He would have to put the mold some place that they had not looked in. But they'd looked everywhere. They had searched the whole house, except for Albert's room. And he didn't want the blame.

Both boys thought and thought. Finally, Otis snapped his fingers. "Trouble with you, Albert, you are not sneaky enough. Here's what to do."

He told Albert. Albert laughed.

"That's a good idea." Albert lay back on the bed. "I'll have to wait until everyone is asleep, though," he said. He closed his eyes, and suddenly Otis was shaking him.

"Listen," Otis said, "why not let me put them back? No one can see me, and we won't have to wait."

"Good idea," Albert said, and then knew it wouldn't work. "You don't know exactly where they were. I do. Sally showed us a thousand times today. Besides, suppose someone saw those plaster teeth floating through the air? That would be the end, the real end."

The next morning, Albert was wakened by Sally's excited scream.

"My teeth! Look, they're right here!"

Albert gathered himself up and went downstairs.

"Where did you find them?" Albert said innocently.

"On the shelf, right on the shelf where they were supposed to be."

"Impossible," Albert said. "We looked there."

"I know. But some books had fallen down, and when I picked them up, there was the mold, right there, Albert."

"Girls," Albert said, in as disgusted a tone as he could manage. "You must have looked right at them a hundred times and you didn't see them."

"But they weren't there yesterday. You looked yourself, Albert."

"They must have been, unless you think they can walk."

Sally turned to her parents, who had come downstairs to see the miracle. "They were here all the time," she said. "They must have been."

Mr. Shook took the plaster mold from Sally and turned it over thoughtfully. Then he gave it back. "Put them in the box, Sally, and take them back to the doctor today." He walked toward the kitchen then, but not before he stopped to stare at Albert. Albert tried to look completely innocent.

"I didn't take them," he said. "Honestly, I didn't." And that was honest, too, he thought, as he ran upstairs to get dressed. He just wished his father hadn't given him that look. His father was awful smart. His mother was smart, too, but she wouldn't think about anything as weird as ghosts. She didn't believe in them. His father was another matter. His father always said there were more things in the world than are dreamed of in your philosophy, Horatio—that was Shakespeare—and claimed that anything was possible.

Albert turned the radio on and Otis woke up, snapped his fingers and materialized.

"She find them?" he asked.

"Of course she found them. And boy, are they all confused. I'll have to do something to take their minds off plaster teeth, I guess. Something they don't expect." He leaned over to tie his shoestrings. "Something responsible. Something—ah." He straightened up and hurried to check his money box. "If I have enough money, I'll fix those windows. At least, I will as soon as Carrie shows me how," he said.

Chapter 6

Ghost Hunting

Albert wiped the putty knife on his jeans and stepped back to admire the new windows in the garage.

"Good job," Carrie said. "Maybe we should start a business, putting windows in."

"Yeah." Albert grinned. He was broke again, but the glass was fixed. He turned just in time to see his volley ball flying through the air.

"Catch, Albert!"

He caught. Clutching the ball he fell to the ground and glared at where he supposed Otis was. "That was really dumb, Otis."

"But I wasn't aiming at the window. I threw it at you."

"Same difference, where I was standing," Albert said. Sometimes, having Otis around was a pain. But most of the time it wasn't. It was a little bit like having a brother. Just a little bit. The thing was that sooner or later Otis was going to do something that would get Albert in a whole mess of trouble—the kind of trouble there was no getting out of. And that made Albert very nervous. On the other hand, Albert had gotten sort of used to having Otis around. There was a chance that he'd miss him. What he really wanted was to have Otis nearby, but not *too* nearby.

Albert kept trying to talk Otis into moving out of the house. "The tree house," he suggested one day. "The rain wouldn't bother you."

Otis said it would, too.

"Then how about the garage? You like the car so much, you could sleep in it."

"And get tossed out each time your mother drove away? I like it here just fine," Otis said.

Sometimes at night Rags came down from the upper bunk and slept on Albert's feet. That wasn't cozy; it made his feet cold. Albert always chased him up to Otis again.

As the summer grew warmer, Albert's room stayed cool. Mr. Shook couldn't understand that, and came often to sit and wonder about it.

"Amazing, that insulation," he would say.

"I know. Really amazing," Albert answered each time.

Now he rolled over on the ground and threw the ball back to where he hoped Otis was. He laughed when it stopped in mid-air and sailed toward Carrie.

"Albert!" His mother stood on the steps, staring. "You're wanted on the phone—but how did you do that? That ball simply turned itself around and—" Mrs. Shook took a firm hold on the railing. "Can you do that again?"

"Sure. It's my special curve ball, Mom." He hurried up the steps and into the house before she could ask another question. Or make him do it again.

Brian was on the phone.

"Thought you weren't speaking to me. Thought you were going around with the kids on Third Street," Albert said.

"I was. But—well, aren't we best friends, Albert? Why don't you come over?"

"You come over here."

"I asked you first."

"You're still scared."

"I am not scared. Why should I be scared of something you made up? Something not even real."

"If it isn't real, then come on over. Gosh, Brian, if I'm not scared and Carrie isn't scared—" Albert stopped. His mother came around the corner, into the dining room where Albert sat on the floor with the telephone. "You come on over, I'll meet you on the front steps."

He hung up and grinned at his mother.

"What do you know, Brian's coming over," he said.

"Good. I'd begun to think you had a real quarrel."

"Oh, well, he's okay. Just a bit of a baby is all."

Mrs. Shook stopped dusting. "That's an awful thing to say about your best friend. What was it all about?"

Albert wondered what his mother would say if he

told her. Scream, most likely. And then faint. No—she'd probably just send him to a psychiatrist.

"Just a stupid fight, Mom. Nothing special, even. Brian's okay." Albert started for the front door.

"Albert," his mother said, "Is there a stray dog around here? I keep hearing a dog barking, but I've never seen one. . . ."

Albert coughed. "I think so—a terrier or something."

Mrs. Shook nodded slowly. "Good," she said, going back to her dusting.

Albert went out to wait on the front steps.

In a few minutes Albert saw Brian ride around the corner. Albert hoped Otis was out back or upstairs. He hadn't seen a ten-speed bike up close. Albert's old bike was the kind you stopped with your feet.

Brian came to a stop in front of Albert.

"What's the bike for? A quick getaway?" Albert asked.

"Shut up," Brian said, grinning. He propped the bike against the iron stair railing. "Just thought you'd ride uptown with me. I have to take a package to my aunt and stop by the library for my mom."

"I have a flat," Albert said. "Want to walk, instead?"

"Why don't you fix it?"

"I will." But not yet, Albert thought. Otis would start fussing with it right away, if I did. He could just see his old green bike racing around the yard all by itself.

"You never will get a ten-speed if you don't keep the old one going."

"Never will, anyhow. Dad says the old one works fine, so he can't see putting money into a new one."

"Christmas, maybe?"

"Maybe. But that's a long time away."

"Yeah." Brian took the books and packages from the baskets by the rear wheel. He was probably the only kid in the world with baskets on a ten-speed, but his mother sent him on errands, every day. He needed them.

Albert yelled through the screen door to let his mother know where he was going, and they started toward the corner.

Something grabbed Albert's leg and held on.

"Cut that out!" Albert shook his left leg in the air. "Rags, stop that."

Brian turned to stone. At least, it looked as though he did. Albert gave his leg a hard shake and pushed Brian.

"Come on—" they raced across the street and grabbed the lamp post on the corner. Albert laughed. Brian didn't laugh, but he didn't run any further, either.

"What was that?"

"Rags. That dumb dog grabbed my pants."

"Oh." Brian looked thoughtful. They walked half a block before he added, "I didn't see any dog."

"Of course not," Albert said. "I just wish he'd grabbed your pants. They maybe you'd believe me." He thought a minute more and added, "but probably not. You'd probably think I was doing it, even if you could see both my hands."

"Be easier to believe than a dumb ghost dog, grabbing you in broad daylight."

"The thing is they're daytime ghosts. Rags is afraid of the dark." Albert shrugged his shoulders. "You got to believe in a ghost afraid of the dark."

Brian stopped and looked at Albert. He smiled a little, then giggled, and finally he laughed and laughed. He fell on the grass, laughing.

"I give up," he said, at last. "I guess I'll go and meet your ghosts when we get back."

"The trouble is you'll like them." Albert said, sitting down beside Brian. "'And I need some help, because I have to get rid of them."

"How come?"

"If I don't, and my mom finds out, we'd have to move, for one thing. She'd never live in a house with two ghosts. And if she doesn't find out, she'll blame me for all the trouble Otis gets into."

"I can see that." Brian thought for awhile and then said they'd better hurry and deliver the package and go to the library. "That's the place to go, if you need to find out about anything."

But the library didn't help very much. Mrs. Finch, the Children's Librarian, helped them find every book she had on the subject of ghosts, and they sat at one of the round tables for more than an hour, looking for a way to get rid of Otis.

"I don't want to exorcise him out of existence," Albert whispered to Brian. "He likes being a ghost, you see."

Mrs. Finch brought another book to them, and stopped a moment. She was a short, plump lady who always smiled, even when she was shushing people who made too much noise. She would look for anything you wanted, no matter how long it took, too. Now she pushed a curl back of her ear, straightened her glasses on her nose, and said that was the last thing she had about ghosts.

"But why ghosts?" she asked. "You two have never wanted anything like that, before."

"Just curious," Brian said.

"Found a haunted house, have you?"

Albert laughed. "No. At least, not exactly. We just wondered what ghosts did when their house was torn down. Where they could go, you know?"

Mrs. Finch was smart as well as smiling. She pulled a chair out and sat down at the table.

"Are you telling me we'll have a ghost when we move into the new building? A White ghost?"

"Of course not. Even if there were such things, all these books say they don't go into new buildings."

"That's a comfort," she said. "Because there must be ghosts, otherwise why do we have so many books about them?"

"Yeah." Albert grinned at Brian. He'd never thought about that argument. Of course, he hadn't known how many books there were about ghosts.

"When do you think you'll move all this into the new building?" Brian asked.

Mrs. Finch said they should be able to guess that better than she could. "You live right there, you see it every day. They tell us we can move in the week before school starts, but I'm not counting on it. You're sure this ghost of yours has nothing to do with the old White house?"

"Well—" Albert hesitated. "That was what made us wonder about it, you see. When the old house was wrecked, it seemed as though it would be a terrible thing, to be a ghost up in that attic and suddenly not have any attic anymore."

"It would," said Mrs. Finch, and she began to say more but was interrupted by a small girl wanting a book about a curious monkey. She smiled at the boys and went away, holding the little girl's hand.

"Let's get out of here," Albert said. "Mrs. Finch is nice but she asks too many questions."

"Besides that, I don't like the way she looked at us when she talked about moving. I bet she asks us to come and carry books." Outdoors, they walked for a time without talking. Albert was busy thinking about the books they had read.

"None of those ghosts were like Otis," he said, at last. "When Otis is invisible, he's all gone. You can't see anything at all. When he materializes, he looks real. Except in bright sunlight, and then he is sort of, you know, kind of frail looking. And Rags is just the same."

"Can Rags—uh—materialize himself?"

"Mostly he just does it when Otis does. But sometimes he gets excited and appears all of a sudden. I can just see what will happen some night. Mom will drop a ball of yarn, or something, and old Rags will go after it and bark and—be there, you know? Mom would have a heart attack—I've got to do something!" He sounded desperate. He felt desperate.

"I see your point," Brian said. His shiny round face was serious as he thought about the problem. "But what I do not see," he said, suddenly, "is what he was doing all the years between."

"Miss Dolly locked him in the tower room."

Brian's face lit up. "Then we can lock him in the storage room, next to yours."

"Wouldn't work. He walks right through walls, when he wants to. Otis says they stayed because they didn't have anywhere else to go."

"Then let's catch him in a bottle."

"He's not a genie, Brian. He's a ghost. And we'd never get him to go into a bottle, anyhow. Even if he could."

"Doesn't he trust you?"

"Well, I guess I keep saying I have to do something about him. He keeps saying he doesn't want doing to." Albert gave a great sigh. He really liked Otis, but—

"Let's have some ice cream. That will help us think," Brian said. "I have some money."

"I don't. Mine all went for windows." Albert grinned. Actually, he never had any money. Holes in his pocket, he always said. Holes in his head, Sally said.

They bought cones across the street from the new library, then cut over to Brian's front steps to eat them.

Brian didn't want to meet the ghosts until he had finished eating.

"There is one good thing about Otis," Albert said, and stopped to take a great lick of chocolate. When he'd swallowed it, he went on. "I got three B's and an A on my card last time, thanks to him. And my room is neat all the time. I mean ALL the time. That Otis is so neat, you wouldn't believe."

"You mean he picks up your ugly junk?"

"All the time. Says he can't abide a mess."

"Maybe he'd better move in with me," Brian said, and turned pale at the thought.

"He couldn't. He can't go off the property."

They finished the cones and Albert told Brian to come on, he had to meet Otis. Brian looked as though he wished he hadn't promised, but then said he had to get his bike anyhow.

"Your bike! Ohmigosh, I forgot about your bike. Let's go!" Albert raced for the corner, and Brian, not so fast, followed.

"What do you mean about my bike?" he yelled.

"Nothing, I hope," shouted Albert over his shoulder. He raced across the street and under the trees that still edged Miss Dolly's yard, until he could see his own front steps. Then he pulled to a stop. Brian stopped just behind him, so close that Albert almost lost his balance.

"I was afraid of that," he said. The bike was gone.

Chapter 7

Otis Takes a Ride

"There he is!" Albert shouted. He raced through the bushes and around the side of the house. Brian followed close behind.

Albert stopped short and Brian almost knocked him over again.

"Hey, that's my bike!"

Brian's bike rode in a circle around the yard, all by itself. At least, it seemed to be all by itself.

"Stop that!" yelled Brian, and pushed past Albert. He grabbed at the bike and jumped back when the bike shot past.

"Can't stop it," yelled Otis. "How do you make it stop?"

"The brakes," shouted Albert. "Hit the brakes!"

"They don't work. I'm trying—"

66

Brian rushed forward again and the bike veered toward the street, went down the drive beside the house. Albert and Brian raced after it, yelling. Rags appeared suddenly, barking and running beside the bike.

"Your hands," Albert yelled, but it was too late. The bike reached the street, gave a lurch and careened out in front of a car. Brakes screeched, the car stopped and a man—a tall and furious man—got out. He stomped around and glared at the boys.

"I've a mind to call the police!" His face quivered with rage. "What kind of games you kids playing? I mighta run right over that bike."

"Yessir," said Albert. Brian lifted the bike and pushed it to the edge of the lawn. "It was an accident," Albert said.

"I'll say it was. Might have been a bad accident." The man still quivered. Albert guessed he was scared as well as mad.

"I was teaching my friend to ride," Albert said. "He fell off, you see."

"Fell off? I didn't see—"

"Yes, and the bike got away." Albert smiled at the man, his very best smile. "We're sorry, honest we are. It was an accident."

"Okay, okay, no harm done. But do your practicing away from the street, hear?" The man got into his car and drove away.

Brian leaned on his bike, shaking his head. "I didn't know you could lie so good."

"Neither did I."

They turned toward the house and faced Albert's mother. She stood on the doorstep, her face white with shock.

"I saw that," she said. "You boys could have been killed."

Albert looked at Brian. She couldn't have seen the whole thing. "Mom, we weren't even on the bike, we didn't ride it in front of that car, honest."

"Yeah, Mrs. Shook, we didn't."

She wasn't listening. "Each time I think you're growing up, you do something dangerous or irresponsible. Or stupid," she added, and turned into the house, letting the screen door slam behind her.

Albert sighed. "You see why I have to do something? Otis didn't mean any harm, you know. He never does."

They went to the tree house, climbed up onto the platform and settled down to wait for Otis. They talked about the last couple of weeks, the end of school, and suddenly Brian shivered.

"Cold up here," he said.

"Good," said Albert.

"What do you mean, good? It can't be this cold in June."

"That's our ghostly air-conditioner," Albert told him. "Otis, Brian wants to meet you."

Brian scrambled up onto his knees. His eyes opened wide. "Where is he? Is he here?"

"Sure. Come on, Otis. Brian isn't mad at you."

"Is that a true fact?" Otis's voice came from above. Both boys looked up. He sat on a branch over their heads.

"He isn't mad, come on down," Albert said. As Otis and Rags settled in a corner of the platform, he added, "but he ought to be. Me too. What a dumb thing to do, Otis."

"Well, your bike has a flat tire," Otis reminded him. "Why wouldn't it stop? My feet went around in circles when I pushed the brakes."

"You don't push with your feet to stop that bike. You squeeze your hands."

"Oh." Otis thought about that. "I thought the handles were funny looking. Did the bike get hurt?"

"No, but that was just lucky. It almost got run over. This is my friend Brian," Albert said.

"I know." Otis looked at Brian, and Brian's face turned red. "Don't be scared. I'm not a bit scary, honest. I'm sorry if I hurt your bike."

"I—it's okay," Brian said, stuttering just a little.

"I was supposed to get a new bike for my birthday. It was already up in the carriage house, waiting. I saw it." Otis leaned forward, his eyes sparkling. "A Napoleon!"

"A what?" asked Albert.

"A Napoleon. You never heard of that? Best bike in the Sears catalog, it was. More than fifteen dollars, too." Otis hugged Rags. "Never got to ride it, though." He rocked back and forth, then looked at Brian. "What makes your face shine like that?"

Albert laughed. "It's his mother. She keeps making him wash his face."

"Is that a joke?"

"No, that's the truth. She says I get dirty fast, and she keeps saying, 'Brian, wash your face.' You use as much soap as I do in a day, your face would shine, too."

"Hey, I'm coming up!" Carrie's voice came first, and then she heaved herself up onto the platform. "Just came from the dentist," she announced. "Ugh, I wouldn't want to spend every day of my life looking into people's mouths." She saw Brian and whistled. "Thought you'd give in pretty soon," she said.

"Well, heck—" Brian's face went red again. "I got lonesome. I got to wondering what you all were doing."

"Carrie explains things to me," Otis said. "I know how almost everything works now. But that television, I'm not so sure about that. I mean, she said that—"

"Never mind. I know how to turn it off and how to turn it on," Brian said. "That's good enough for me."

"Yes, but there's this box and if you press the button the picture will change, clear across the room. That's pretty good, I think. My pa—

Albert interrupted. "You mean MY pa, if you ever go and do it when he's around. He's the one who would have sixteen fits. That remote control thing is his toy, he says." Albert sounded cross, but only because he was afraid.

"You don't need to worry, I won't do anything to it," Otis said.

"Of course he won't," Carrie agreed. "Stop fussing and let's ride up to the park."

"I can't," Otis said.

"Oh, that's right." Carrie laughed and shook her head. "Why can't I remember that?"

"Listen, Rags and me are going out front and watch the cars," Otis said. "We kind of like to do that, you know. You go ride in the park. We'll see you when you get back."

They disappeared. After a moment, Brian scrambled up onto his knees. "Is he really gone?"

"I don't know." Albert grinned. "You can't exactly tell. But it doesn't feel as cold now, does it? So probably he is gone."

"He's the nicest ghost I ever knew," Carrie said. The boys laughed.

"He's the only ghost you ever knew," Albert told her. "Come on, let's go fix my flat."

When they came back from riding, they stopped on Second street in front of Miss Dolly's yard. They propped their bikes and sat on the wall, facing the new building, so that they could watch the builders. Rags materialized suddenly, and landed on Carrie's lap.

They could hear Otis, but they couldn't see him.

"You ought to see the insides," he said. "I don't see why they need such big rooms."

"Because they have a lot of books," Albert said. "Mrs. Finch told me there are twenty thousand books in the Children's Room, when they're all there. Of course, they never are all there."

Otis snapped his fingers and materialized, sitting on the ground in front of Albert. "You don't mean twenty thousand, Albert. Aren't that many books anywhere."

"You just wait and see." From the corner of his eye he saw movement inside the new building, and he jumped down and sat beside Otis, hiding him. "My gosh, Otis, suppose someone saw you appear like that? You shouldn't do it, not out here."

"I forgot," Otis said. "I get tired of remembering all the time."

"Ah, Otis—" Albert started to put his arm around Otis's shoulder, then changed his mind. "Listen, we were up at the library today, there's a lot of books about ghosts, you know."

"There are?"

"Sure. And most of them said ghosts come around because they are still mad about something. You mad, Otis? You want revenge?"

"Of course not. Why would I want revenge? I had a birthday coming, didn't I? And my Napoleon."

"Your what?" asked Carrie.

"His new bike," Brian explained. "I don't guess you'd want to be a ghost just because you didn't get your bike, would you? Anyhow, you can ride Albert's."

"No you can't! At least, not in the daytime, Otis."

"Look, no one knows for absolute sure about ghosts," Carrie said. "So why don't you stop worrying about it?" Carrie giggled. "You are probably a ghost because you are so curious about everything. And you hadn't found all the answers when that horse landed on you."

"That sounds logical," Otis said. "But how long—"

"Just forget it, Otis. You don't have any trouble forgetting not to get in trouble, so why can't you forget about why you are a ghost?"

"But, Albert—"

"Hope they leave this wall up," Carrie interrupted. "This is where we sit to watch the parade on Fourth of July."

"Does a parade come right by here?"

"Of course it does. Every parade comes right past here."

"Didn't you ever hear the bands playing, up in your attic, Otis?" Albert asked.

Otis shook his head. "Didn't hear anything. I sure wasted a lot of time, all those years," he said. He stuck his thumbs behind his suspender straps and pulled at them. He leaned back and smiled up at the tree above his head. "We used to have the best Fourths," he said, in a dreamy sort of voice. "We had the band playing up at the park, and speeches and food. Everyone had a picnic, right up in front of the town hall. Best food you ever tasted."

"What do you mean, everyone? The whole town?"

"Practically, I think. Big long tables and everyone's

mother cooked the best they knew how. The speeches were in the morning, of course, before we ate. My pa said you could work up quite an appetite listening to a congressman in the morning."

"Was that fun?"

"Sure it was." Otis's blue eyes sparkled. "One time Pud and me swiped a basket from the back of his pa's buggy, and we hid underneath and ate a whole chocolate cake. Mrs. Harris could bake the best chocolate cake, I'll tell you. We were glad the speeches were long, that day. Takes a good while to eat a whole cake."

"Pud? Pud Harris?" Albert searched his memory. "I know! That would be the Paul Harris that Miss Dolly said cried for three days when that horse got you."

"Pud did? Gosh!" Otis looked surprised.

"Would Pud Harris be Paul Harris?" Carrie asked.

"Sure he would be. Only we always called him Pud. Can't remember why, but we did."

"Well, he always rides in the first car in every parade."

"Not Pud," Otis protested. "He wouldn't ride. He'd march with the band or something."

Carrie said that Mr. Harris marched in the parades until he was eighty. "When he was eighty, he said he was old enough to ride. He's one of the oldest folks in town and he was Mayor longer than anyone else, Miss Dolly said."

"If he's going to be in the parade, I don't want to miss it. Can we sit right here?"

"Of course we can," Carrie said.

Albert felt uncomfortable, all of a sudden. He wished he had never mentioned Pud Harris. He wished he'd forgotten what Miss Dolly told him.

For the first time in his life, Albert dreaded the Fourth of July.

Chapter 8

Pud in the Parade

Dreading the Fourth of July did not stop it from coming. The only thing interesting that happened before that day happened at the new library. Someone got in at night and did a lot of damage.

"We think it was kids," the policeman said. "They broke every window on the north side, glass all over everywhere. They knocked down piles of wood, and poured cement all over the place." He'd stopped by to see if anyone in the Shook family had heard anything. "You living so close," he said, and looked at Albert.

Albert said, "Listen, I wouldn't do that." He was glad when his family backed him up.

"You may be careless and lack a sense of responsibility," his mother said, later, "but I know you aren't a vandal."

"Thanks, I guess," Albert said. She was still worried about that bike thing, he knew.

They didn't catch the vandals, and Albert didn't tell Otis about them. He knew Otis wasn't guilty. At first, he'd thought—but no. Otis could not abide a mess, so he wouldn't go around making one. Albert was sure of that.

The day after the third was the fourth, same as every year, and Albert woke up to the sound of firecrackers. They weren't allowed in Ohio, but some kids always had them just the same.

"Listen to that!" Otis was awake; his feet swung down in Albert's face. "Get up, Rags, come on. It's the Fourth of July. Pud's going to be in the parade."

Albert groaned and rolled away. He didn't want Otis to see Pud Harris, but he didn't see how he could stop it.

By ten o'clock, Otis was out on the wall. Albert waited for the cannon shot that meant the parade was starting. When he heard it, he hurried out. If he stayed right there he could stop Otis from doing anything dumb.

Brian and Carrie were on the wall already, with a space between them. Three flags were waving in the air, one of them all by itself.

"Hey, you can't do that!" Albert shouted, and grabbed for the flag. Otis pulled it back and Albert fell onto the ground, rolling back and forth grabbing at the flag until Carrie jumped down and sat on him.

"Ooof!" He yelled, and this time caught the flag.

Carrie bounced on him and told him to stop. "People will think you are nuts," she hissed.

He realized, then, what she meant. Neighbors, sitting on the tree lawn waiting for the parade, were all looking at them and smiling. "They'll think I'm having a fit," he said. "Fighting with myself, oh gosh—" but he had the flag, now. He dumped Carrie and sat up, laughing. "They'll think you're an awful tomboy, landing on me like that."

"So what's new?" Carrie said.

Albert laughed. "Listen, Otis, you can't go waving a flag," he said.

"But it's the Fourth of July," Otis protested.

"But you can't—" Albert gave up. No sense arguing with Otis. He sat on the wall beside Carrie. The band came around the corner, and all heads turned to watch. Saved by the band, Albert thought.

"Wowee!" Otis yelled, as the band went by. "Watch that drummer!"

The drum sticks flew high into the air. The drummer caught them without missing a step.

"Here come the cars. Is that Pud? Is it?"

"In the first one, Otis."

"No, that can't be Pud." Otis sounded bewildered. A thin, old man sat up on the open back of the first car. When he saw the children, he waved his straw hat and then, quick as could be, he rolled it up his arm and flipped it onto his head.

"That's Pud! He always loved that trick! Hey, Pud!"

Otis materialized, and a boy in checkered pants and wide, black suspenders dashed along the sidewalk, yelling and waving his arms.

"Pud! It's me, Otis White!"

Mr. Harris stood up on the seat, turning as the car went slowly past. His mouth opened, and his face grew as white as his hair.

"It's me, Pud! Otis! Hey, Pud!"

The car slowly carried Mr. Harris past the corner. Otis stopped running and stood waving. Mr. Harris waved, then, he waved and waved while he stared back at Otis. The people in the next block waved at him.

Otis walked slowly back to the wall and sat down.

"Do you think he saw me?"

"Everyone saw you," Albert said. He was sitting with his eyes closed. What would happen now?

"If anyone asks, you are my cousin from Cleveland," Carrie told Otis.

But no one asked. No one had paid any attention to one more boy shouting, even a boy in checkered knee pants and suspenders.

Otis wanted to stay on the wall after the parade.

"Pud will come back," he insisted.

Albert said he wouldn't. "They have a festival, a carnival like, up at the park. Old cars and games and stuff. Mr. Harris will have to stay there. Listen, you just stay here if you want to. We're going up to the park anyhow, after lunch. I'll look for him."

Otis disappeared.

"Hey, you can't do that," Albert shouted.

"I did it. I don't see why I can't go to the park. I'm sick of being a ghost."

"Where'd that kid go? The one in the funny pants?" A strange man stood beside Albert, holding a green folding chair.

"Over the wall," Carrie said, before Albert could find an answer. "He rolled over the wall. Why? Do you want him?"

"I don't want him, but—he was there and then—" the man rubbed his hand across his eyes. "I will swear he was there."

"He was," Albert said. "But like Carrie told you, he rolled over the wall. He's gone home now."

The man muttered something and walked up the street. Albert, Carrie and Brian watched him until he was three houses away. Then they sank down in a row on the wall.

"Close one," Brian said.

"I told you, Otis. You've got to be more careful."

Carrie said it was dumb. "Just stupid, Otis, to disappear like that, right out here on Second Street. All these people still around across the street, my gosh, Otis."

Otis didn't answer. Albert turned around, swung his legs on the library side of the wall.

"Otis?"

No answer.

Carrie sighed. "When he goes, he's gone," she said, and the boys laughed.

"Hope he stays away for the whole day," Albert said

in a loud voice. "I have to do something about him."

A branch over their heads swung down, just missing Albert, and he jumped up. "Hah! I knew you were still here, Otis. Come on, let's go home. I was only joking."

"You go home," Otis said, from somewhere. "I don't feel so good, Albert. I think I have a problem." He snapped his fingers, and nothing happened. "See?"

"I don't see anything."

"That's what I mean. Nothing happened when I snapped my fingers. Even old Rags—"

"Oh—oh my gosh, Otis. You said you were sick of being a ghost! You said it, and now you can't materialize. You got to do something, quick. You said—"

"Yes, but I'm not sick of it yet, Albert. I want to talk to Pud. I want to be a ghost."

"Keep saying it, then. Keep saying you want to be a ghost." Albert felt as though he was fading away himself. "Keep saying it, Otis!"

"I want to be a ghost, I want to be a ghost—" Otis snapped his fingers and was suddenly there, on the branch over their heads. He grinned. "That was a close one for me," he said. "I feel better now, though. I'll just sit here and wait for Pud."

"He won't be able to come today, Otis. Honest." Albert started for home. Carrie told Otis to please stay a ghost. Even Brian told him to keep on wanting, before he followed the others.

"You missed your chance, though, Albert," he said then. "If you'd kept quiet, Otis might have disappeared for good."

"I know. But I couldn't do that to Otis, now could I?"

As they turned the corner, they heard Otis shouting after them. "You don't have to do nothing about me, Albert. I like it fine, just the way I am."

At the park that afternoon, Albert looked around for Mr. Harris. Half the town was there, either running the games or playing them. The money was for a new bandstand, one that would look just like the old one which burned down a long time ago. They had drawings of it propped against the fish pond railing. Mr. Harris sat there, too, holding a cane and talking to people as they strolled by. He looked small, Albert thought. He looked bothered. He kept staring off into space, right when people were talking to him. Then he'd rub his forehead and nod. And smile.

"Mr. Harris?" Albert got up close and waited for a lady in pink to say hello and move on. He inched closer.

"Mr. Harris? Listen, could you come and visit Otis?"

The old man sat still as a stone for a moment, then slowly turned his head and looked at Albert. "What's your name?" he asked, finally.

"Albert Shook, sir. Listen—"

"Albert? You listen. I don't know anyone named Otis. I haven't known anyone named Otis for—"

"But you used to, didn't you?"

"Certainly, I used to. I also liked playing pranks on my elders, but that doesn't mean I like them played on me."

"Please listen, sir." Albert told about Otis moving into his attic room when the house was wrecked. Mr. Harris listened, his eyes fixed on Albert's face. He didn't even blink.

Then he said, "Nonsense."

"I know it sounds like nonsense, but it isn't. Every word is true," Albert insisted.

"Albert, you have a large imagination. Too large. There are no such things as—"

"Yes, there are. Just come down and sit on the wall in front of the new library building. Come tomorrow. Otis wants to talk to you."

"Ridiculous," said Mr. Harris. He tapped his cane on the sidewalk. "Silliest thing I ever heard. Do you know how old I am?"

"Yes, sir. Eighty-seven, same as Otis."

"I've lived eighty-seven years without once meeting a ghost. Why should I start seeing them now?"

"But you did see one this morning, didn't you?"

Some people came by and stopped to talk to Mr. Harris. When the people walked away, Albert took a few steps away, too.

"You don't sound like the Pud Harris I heard about," he said, looking back. "You don't sound like any kid who would swipe his own mother's chocolate cake and eat it all up, hiding under a wagon."

Mr. Harris stopped tapping his cane. He stared at Albert, squinting his eyes in the sunlight. "Wasn't a wagon," he said. "It was a buggy. The buggies were lined up for two blocks that day."

"Albert, there you are!" Mrs. Shook stood smiling at them. "Good afternoon, Mr. Harris."

Albert jumped up beside his mother, making faces at Mr. Harris, trying to tell him not to mention Otis. He must have caught on, all right, for he chatted with Mrs. Shook about the old bandstand.

"I played trombone with the Fireman's band when I was a kid," he said. "Bandstand was right over there." He pointed with his cane.

When they walked away a few minutes later, Mr. Harris called after them. "Think I'd better come down, see how the new library is doing. Mebbe tomorrow I'll do that."

Albert grinned. "That's a good idea," he said. But he wasn't sure it was. It might make Otis miserable instead of happy. Being host to a ghost was not an easy job.

Chapter 9

Camp and Cars

The day after the fourth, it rained.

"Pourin' cats and dogs," Otis muttered. "Looks as though it won't ever stop."

Albert was glad.

"Maybe Mr. Harris will forget," he said, but he didn't believe it.

"He won't. My gosh, Albert, would you forget the first ghost you ever saw, which was me?"

Albert laughed. He wouldn't forget Otis, not in a million years.

The next day the sun came out. Otis, Albert and Carrie waited by the wall all morning, watching. Finally Albert and Carrie went home for lunch. When they came back Mr. Harris was sitting there. Otis wasn't in sight.

"Well, Albert Shook," Mr. Harris greeted him. He was smiling, and his small dark eyes were filled with fun. "Not many people by here today, but those that were, they think old man Harris is failing fast, sitting here talking to himself." He thought that was funny, and chuckled. Albert grinned, too, and introduced Carrie.

"Otis is real, see? I wasn't kidding you." Albert perched on the wall, hugging his knees. "He's a ghost, but—"

"Don't talk about me as if I wasn't here," Otis said.

"Well, don't materialize," Albert begged. "Not out here."

"I won't." But Rags did, jumping into Carrie's lap and licking her face. Mr. Harris leaned back, surprised.

"Why, Otis," he said. "That's Rags, it really is."

"I know that. Told you so. Honest, Pud, I don't think you believe in me yet. Tell me about Jimmy Burt, what did he grow up to be?"

Mr. Harris chuckled some more, and shrugged his shoulders toward Albert. "He must be real," he whispered.

"Of course I am," Otis answered.

So Mr. Harris told Otis about all their old friends, and Carrie and Albert listened. They didn't know many of the people, but at least they could sit there, Albert figured, so Mr. Harris wouldn't look as though he was failing fast, sitting there talking to himself.

"I'll be back," he promised, when he finally stood

up. The children watched as he walked down the street, stepping carefully. When he came to the corner he turned and waved his cane at them.

That night, Otis told Albert about Mr. Harris's arrival.

"He walked along, real slow, as though he didn't quite want to come. Then he stood by the wall and said my name real quiet like. I said, 'Hey, Pud,' and he jumped. Bet he jumped three feet. Then he laughed."

Otis laughed, too. "He looks just like his own grandpa, Albert. He says he was on the library board for twenty years, so people won't think anything of him coming to sit on the wall and watch the builders. Says he goes walking every day, anyhow. That's how he's lived so long, he says."

Otis was quiet for a moment, then he added, "But Albert, imagine old Pud on the library board. He never even liked to read."

"He grew up, that's what happened, Otis."

"Yeah. Think I'd a been on the library board, if I'd grown up?"

"Sure. You like to read right now, don't you?"

"That's so," Otis said, and he settled down to sleep. A moment later, he said, "Anyhow, Albert, Pud doesn't know how long a person stays a ghost, either. No one knows."

The next morning, Albert's mother said they had to get his clothes ready for camp.

"Camp?" Albert had forgotten about that. "I can't go to camp!"

"What are you talking about, Albert? We sent the money in last spring, remember? What a silly thing to say."

"But I can't. I forgot about it, and I can't."

"Better start remembering, dear. It was all you could talk about last winter. You begged for a month at camp. A whole month, remember?"

"Yes, but—" Albert couldn't explain. He couldn't leave Otis, though. He didn't see how he could.

But a week later, he did. He went to a camp fifty miles away in a big woods, with a swimming pool and cabins and a hundred and forty other boys, and he worried about Otis each day. He couldn't write to him, could he? He couldn't call. Imagine saying, "Hi, Mom, let me speak to Otis."

Then, on the first Friday, the senior counselor yelled at Albert just as he came up for air after a perfect dive. "Long distance, Albert. From Otis White."

Albert gasped and hurried to the office.

"Listen, when are you coming home?" Otis asked, first thing.

"Otis? Is that really you?" Albert shook the water from his ears. "How did you know how to dial?"

"Carrie showed me last week before she went to her Grandma's. When are you coming home?"

"But Otis, is anyone there?"

"Of course no one is here. Is camp almost over?"

"It's only begun." Albert sighed, then shivered. He

was dripping wet. "I have to stay three more weeks, Otis. Are you okay?"

"I guess so. But it isn't much fun with you gone away."

"I can't help it, Otis."

"I know that. But all Rags and me got to do is sit around the library and watch the workmen. Sometimes that's funny, though."

Albert's stomach did a flip-flop. "How funny?" he asked.

"Well, this afternoon a can got knocked over, and Rags pushed it all over the place. I near split laughing, but the man didn't think it was funny. He was chasing it and yelling. He couldn't see Rags, you know, and I'll tell you—" Otis stopped talking to laugh some more.

Albert had to laugh too. He wished he'd been there. "Can't you lock Rags up?"

"Of course not. Something else happened at the library, Albert. Some kids broke in and stole a lot of things. They broke that big window and poured white stuff all over the steps. Helped themselves to a lot of wood, too, your dad says."

"Who says?"

"Your dad. I heard him say it when we were watching television."

Albert's head whirled. "When who was watching television?"

"Everyone—except Rags. I made him stay upstairs because he gets too excited."

"I know." Albert figured his heart was about six

inches into his stomach. He never should have come to camp! "Did they catch the vandals, Otis?"

"The vandals? Oh, you mean the ones who broke in? No, but your dad says they were probably the same ones broke into Watson's house down the street last Tuesday night. Made a mess of that place, too. The Watsons were real upset."

"All the exciting things happen when I'm not at home," Albert said. "We could have caught them, I bet."

"Yeah. Oh, hey, I've got to hang up, Albert. 'General Hospital' is on in a minute."

The line went dead. Albert hung up, too, and went slowly back to the pool. It was sure dangerous, leaving Otis home all alone. And wouldn't his mom wonder about the phone bill, when it came? Albert would have laughed, but it just wasn't that funny.

The next week, his mother wrote that odd things were happening. "I keep hearing your radio," she wrote. "I hear it, but when I go upstairs, it isn't on. Your father says I must miss you, so I'm hearing things. Brian is camping out west."

Albert groaned. No one there for Otis now, but Mr. Harris.

At the end of the long month, his father came for him. All the way home, Albert talked about camp and thought about Otis. As they neared the town limits, Albert ran out of things to tell and Mr. Shook said it was a funny thing.

"What's a funny thing?" Albert asked, although he wasn't sure he wanted to hear the answer.

"Your room, Albert. It's cold up there, for one thing. Your mother keeps hearing your radio. One day—" Mr. Shook paused while he passed a truck. Albert scrootched down in his seat.

"One day," his father went on, "she took some clothes up and saw your books all over the floor and your skulls—"

"What about my skulls?" Albert sat up straight.

"All over the place, she said. But when we went up later, to straighten it up, it was neat again. Everything in its place."

Albert stared out the window. Finally, he said, "I left it neat."

"I know you did. That's why your mother waited for me to go up and see it. At first, I thought it was a poltergeist."

"What's a poltergeist?"

"A ghost who throws things. But I never heard of one who also picks them up."

They drove down Main Street. Albert looked at the familiar stores and was glad to see them, but mostly he was scared for Otis.

"I don't think I want to know what is going on, Albert," Mr. Shook said, then. He didn't look at Albert when he spoke. "If I knew, I'd have to do something about it, right? Get an exorcist or something. Find another house."

"I like our house." Albert said quickly.

"So do I. But this kind of thing makes your mother nervous. To say the least." He turned down Second Street. "And I've got to say it makes me nervous," he added.

"Me, too," muttered Albert.

They passed Brian's apartment and turned into their own street just in time to see Mrs. Shook's car backing down the drive. It jerked back and forth and then ploughed across the yard and crashed into the elm tree.

Mr. Shook slammed on the brakes. Albert's mother came running down the drive, a bag of groceries in each arm.

"Stop it!" she yelled, although it was stopped already. "Stop it!"

Mr. Shook stared at the car, and then at Albert.

"There's no one driving it," he said. "Is there?"

Albert was speechless. He couldn't even shake his head. They walked over and strolled all around the car, looking. The fender was bent, but mostly the bumper had done its job. Mr. Shook looked inside.

"Keys in here," he said, and looked at Mrs. Shook. "Are you sure you left it in park?"

"Of course I did." She frowned. "I thought I did. I thought so, but maybe not. I was just unloading the groceries, before I put it in the garage."

"Automatic drive—if you bumped it into reverse when you got out," Mr. Shook began, and looked at Albert. Albert looked at his mother. Then he hugged her, to remind her he was home after a whole month away. She hugged back, forgetting the car for a moment. Then, without being told to do it, he carried his gear from the other car. He spread his sleeping bag across the line to air out, and carried his dirty clothes to the basement. Finally he took his suitcase upstairs. He went into his room and shut the door.

"Otis? You here?"

"Welcome back." Otis materialized on the upper bunk, swinging his legs and looking sheepish.

"Yeah," said Albert. He was surprised how glad he felt, seeing Otis again. Slowly he let a smile come. "That was a dumb stupid thing you did, Otis. Driving Mom's car, my gosh! You could have been killed," he said.

Chapter 10

Albert's Plan

For the second time in an hour, Albert was speechless. He couldn't believe he'd said such a silly thing.

"Now, listen," he said, when they both stopped laughing. "My dad says we have to move to a new house if the funny things don't stop."

"But I like music," Otis said.

"The radio wasn't so bad, but why did you throw my books all over the floor? That wasn't like you, Otis."

"I didn't throw them. I had them open, that's all. I was studying your dumb, old skulls. I drew some pictures, too." He slid off the bunk and pulled some papers from a neat pile. "See?"

Albert said they were good pictures of his skulls, but why did Otis pick up the books, after his mother saw them?

"But I didn't know she'd seen them. It was time for Pud to come, and I went out to talk to him. When I came back, I straightened it all up. You know, Albert, I can't abide a mess." Otis sighed and floated up to the top bunk. "They came upstairs just after I'd finished, and boy, I'll tell you, they got upset. Your ma screamed and said all kinds of things."

"I'll bet she did. What did Dad say?"

"He kept saying are you sure they were on the floor? He said it so many times she wasn't sure after a while."

"Poor Mom."

"Yeah. I'm real sorry. But you know, Albert, I can't—"

"You can't abide a mess. I know."

"Well, it's true." Otis jumped down from the top bunk. "Come on, I want to show you what they've done to the new building."

Albert hurried through the back yard and pushed his way through the hedge. Otis chattered all the way, even though he was invisible.

"Carrie says the parking lot has to be blacktopped, Albert. What's a black top?"

"Ask Carrie," Albert said, and ran up to peer into the library windows. Otis went right through.

"Come on in," he called. Albert shook his head in disgust.

"How can I do that?"

"Oh." Otis materialized and looked out. He laughed. "I forgot you have to use the door. And it's locked, I guess. It's Saturday." He came back through the glass and stood beside Albert. Then he disappeared. "People on the other side," he explained.

Albert grinned. Otis was getting smarter, he thought. He peered in the next window. "Awful lot of shelves," he said. "And junk."

"Not junk. Paint cans and stuff. I wanted to help them paint awful bad, but I didn't."

Albert thought about that, and shivered. He could see a paint brush painting walls all by itself and all the workers running out of the building.

"Otis," he began, but Otis interrupted and said it was time for Pud to come. They went around to the wall and Albert sat down. He had an idea, and he thought maybe it was a good one.

When Mr. Harris came, Albert told them all about camp. Mr. Harris and Otis both said they never heard of camps like that when they were twelve.

"Reminds me of the picnic we had in Peer's Wood," Otis said.

"And that skunk came along—" and they were off, talking about when they were boys. Albert listened, but mostly he thought about his idea. When Mr. Harris left, Albert followed him across the street, where Otis couldn't go. He explained his idea.

"Makes sense," Mr. Harris said.

The next afternoon Brian and Carrie helped Albert make a sheltered space in the back yard. They used a big packing box that was in the garage, dragged it out and made a wall with it. When Mr. Harris came, they gave him a folding chair to sit on. Then Carrie went to look for Otis.

"What's that?" Otis asked when she brought him to the back yard.

"That's so you can talk to Mr. Harris and he can see you, Otis. Out front you never can materialize, can you?"

"No, but—"

"Come on, Otis. No one can see you."

Otis materialized. He hugged his checkered knees and grinned at Mr. Harris. Mr. Harris grinned back. He pulled a white handkerchief out and wiped his eyes.

"Well, Otis," he said. They talked about a lot of things and then Mr. Harris said they'd had an idea.

Albert held his breath.

"You and Rags have to find a good home," Mr. Harris said. "It seems to me—"

"Now, listen," Otis interrupted, glaring at Albert. Mr. Harris waved his cane.

"You listen first, Otis. The new library has a second floor that won't be used for books or people at all. Just fans and a little storage. You and Rags could be very comfortable up there."

"In the library? It's brand new!" Otis made a face.

"That isn't so bad, being all new. The thing is, Otis, they will have all the newspapers there, from before we were born and all the years since then. You put them on this film reader and press the button, and you can read the paper."

Otis looked puzzled. "The newspaper on film? Is that a true fact, Carrie?"

"Sure it is, Otis. Magazines, too. You could read about everything, at the library."

"Yes, and you could read all the books. You've probably finished all of mine," Albert said.

"Hmmmm," said Otis.

"You could learn to work the computer and the copy machine, too," Carrie said. "You remember I told you about them."

"Hmmmmm," said Otis.

Brian leaned forward. "Listen, my mom says one of the rooms will have pictures all around it, pictures taken when you were a kid, Otis. You could go and look at them every day."

"And there will be people there all the time," Carrie said. "You wouldn't get lonesome."

Otis pulled a bunch of grass and twisted it around his fingers. "I couldn't talk to them," he said. "Just think about that. What if I forgot and talked to someone? Or if I materialized?"

"You wouldn't do that." Albert thought a moment. "Would you?"

"Of course you wouldn't," Mr. Harris said. "If people got the notion the library was haunted, that would be terrible. You wouldn't do that."

Albert wasn't so sure. If Otis didn't, Rags might. But he said they would come to visit nearly every day. "You could whisper to us. And nothing to stop you from coming out to the tree house, after all."

"But not any further," Mr. Harris said. "Albert's house would be off limits."

Otis thought about it. He twisted the grass and let it drop from his fingers. He pulled a suspender strap and let it snap back into place.

"Any pictures of me, in that room?"

"We don't know. It isn't opened yet, silly."

"There will be," Mr. Harris said. "Our school picture in 1902, Otis, taken on the school step. Remember?"

"That settles it," Otis said. "When they get it done, I'll go see it. I'll probably go every day. But I like your room, Albert. I can live there just fine."

"But Otis," Carrie exclaimed, "you can't stay there. We told you, Mr. Shook said they would have to move. Do you want Albert to move?"

"My mom is all upset, Otis. You can't stay with us any longer. She's beginning to ask questions, and—"

"I'll be real careful, honest I will. But I like the music and I like you, Albert."

"But, Otis—" Albert stopped. He ran his fingers through his hair and sighed. "I like you, Otis, we all like you. But you just don't seem to remember that you're a ghost."

"Sure I do." Otis disappeared. "See? I'm a ghost. I won't be any trouble. I'll sleep at your house and I will go to the library every day when you go to school." When they called him, he didn't answer.

After a while, Mr. Harris said they would try again the next day. He walked slowly down the driveway.

Albert sat with his chin on his knees. He felt awful. "It isn't that I don't want Otis in my room," he said.

"We know that." Brian looked glum, too. Then his face brightened. "Listen, we haven't slept out all summer. Let's sleep in the tree house tonight."

"Tonight?" Albert scrambled to his feet. "Good idea, let's ask," he said. As he ran to the house he thought that if they slept out, he wouldn't have to argue with Otis. Unless Otis slept out, too.

Chapter 11

To the Rescue

Otis didn't want to sleep out.

"Why do you want to do that, when you have this good old bed right here?"

Albert looked up at him. "Guess you are eighty-seven years old, if you don't like sleeping out," he said. He gathered his sleeping bag and flashlight and said goodnight to Otis. He stopped in the kitchen to pick up a sack of cookies and some apples.

"We'll leave the kitchen light on," his mother said, "just in case you want something or it rains."

"It's not going to rain tonight," Mr. Shook said. "Those aren't rain clouds." He looked up at the sky and added that he hoped they weren't rain clouds.

Albert hoped that, too. They never had put a roof on the tree house.

Brian was already on the platform, sitting on his sleeping bag and eating cookies, when Albert pushed his stuff through the hole. He climbed up, spread his sleeping bag, and then leaned his elbows on the railing and looked out at the new building.

"Remember Miss Dolly's house? We could always pretend it was a castle, or something. You can't pretend about that library. It's just a big square."

"All those towers cost money." Brian finished the last cookie and crawled into his bag. Then he came out again, pulled his shoes off, and pushed them into a corner. Albert took his shoes off, too.

They talked until it was really dark and then they read comic books by flashlight. Finally they turned the lights off, and moments later the ladder scraped against the tree. The boys froze, until they heard Carrie's voice.

"Didn't think you'd be asleep already," she said, and crawled up onto the platform. "Brought you some birthday cake."

"How did you get out?" Albert sat up and turned on his flashlight. He reached for some cake. He could always eat cake.

"By the back door, of course. My folks are watching TV in bed, so I'd better not stay long. They might miss me."

"Or the cake. Whose birthday?" Brian asked.

"My mother's. They won't miss the cake. She said it was foolish to have a cake at her age."

"It's never foolish to have cake," Brian said, licking his fingers.

Carrie stepped over Albert and crouched down, looking over the railing toward the library. "I saw a car," she whispered. "They turned out the lights."

The boys reached the railing in time to see the car back out of the library driveway.

"Just turning around, that's all," Albert said. They settled down again. Carrie stood by the railing.

"Someone is over there," she insisted, in a whisper.

"Where?"

"At the library, dummy. I saw someone move in the bushes. Honest. In the shadows."

"You're making it up. Go home," Albert said. "Thanks for the cake."

"But I did see someone."

"Listen, go home. Flick the back light so we'll know you got there."

"You could at least come and look," she whispered.

"No, I couldn't. I'm comfortable."

"If someone is there, you may need me."

"Carrie, no one is there. But if we need you, believe me, we'll come and flash our light at your window. You can call the police, okay?"

"Oh—" Carrie sounded disgusted, but she slipped down the ladder and a few seconds later the back porch light flicked on and off again.

The boys climbed quickly out of their bags and peered through the darkness. Nothing moved, nothing at all. The clouds had moved on, and the moonlight and trees made great shadows on the parking area, but nothing moved.

"Do you think she really saw someone?" Brian asked after a few minutes.

"Of course not. She just wanted to scare us; you know Carrie. Just because she isn't allowed to sleep out, she thinks she can scare us so that we'll go inside." Albert slid into his sleeping bag and pulled the zipper up. He wished he really believed that Carrie would do that. The trouble was, he didn't. She might be mad because she wasn't allowed to sleep out, but she wouldn't be mean.

Albert lay flat on his back and stared into the dark tree branches over his head. Maybe she did see someone. He closed his eyes; they popped open again. For a long time he kept closing his eyes and they kept opening. He started counting the cars he could hear on Second Street, but it was so late they didn't come fast enough. He counted the stars, but the leaves were too thick. He couldn't see many stars. Five, just five stars up there. She couldn't have heard anyone over there, not really. She only made it up, he thought. Then he heard glass breaking.

He sat up, fast. "Brian, you hear that? Someone is over there, all right."

Brian snored. Albert reached out and shook him. "Hey, wake up, someone is over there. Let's go!"

"You're nuts." Brian sat up. He lowered his voice. "You didn't hear anything."

"I did, they broke a window, I heard a window break. They're probably inside already."

"Flash Carrie, she'll call the police." Brian struggled

up to his knees and looked through the darkness. "I don't see anything."

"Of course you don't. It was way on the other side. Come on—" Albert slid out of the tree house and along the branch. He dropped to the ground. Brian came down the ladder, holding his flashlight.

"Go over and signal Carrie," Albert said, giving him a shove. "But be quiet."

"I will." Brian stepped away and then stopped. "What are you going to do?"

"Get Otis, if I can." Albert found some stones and threw one. It went high, and he heard it land with a thump on the far side of the house. He threw again and hit the screen of his bedroom window, this time. Nothing happened.

Albert threw another stone. Plonk, it hit the screen but still nothing happened. Brian came back.

"She turned her lights on," he said.

"Then let's go," Albert said. Brian grabbed his arm.

"Why? The police will come," he whispered. "We'd better stay here, or call your dad or something."

"But they may be gone by then. Come on." Albert slid through the bushes that separated his yard from the library lot. Once on the other side he paused and waited for Brian.

"We'll keep in the shadow," Albert whispered. On tiptoe he edged around the parking lot. Brian came behind. He stumbled on a rock and caught Albert's arm. They stood still, listening. It was awfully dark near the building.

Albert's insides felt hollowed out and he swallowed. It was kind of silly to go after the vandals all alone, just the two of them. But—

"If we don't, they could do a lot of rotten things," he whispered. "Remember those paint cans? We ought to stop them somehow."

"You mean go through the broken window, too?"

"I don't know. I wish I had my shoes on," Albert said.

They crept toward the new building. Then, as they reached the wide side doors, everything happened at once.

A dog barked.

Voices screamed.

The wide doors burst open.

Someone flew through the doorway, turned around once and sprawled on the ground. A familiar voice yelled, "Grab him!"

Albert and Brian grabbed. They sat right down on him and held tight. Car lights flooded the scene as another figure stopped in the doorway and then fell forward, as though someone had tackled it. Albert jumped up and grabbed this one, just as a policeman reached out and yanked the intruder to his feet.

A second policeman pulled the boy from beneath Brian. Carrie, her father and Mr. Shook burst through the bushes.

The dog stopped barking.

For a moment, Albert thought, it was like the end of a TV show. Everyone frozen in place.

Then the taller boy spoke. "I never thought I'd be glad to see a cop," he said. His face was the color of ashes and he couldn't stop shaking and sniffling.

"That other kid, where's he? The one inside—first you'd see him and then—" the second boy shuddered. "Like a ghost he was, in and out of the shadows."

"What other kid?" The policemen looked around and Carrie spoke up quickly.

"You must mean Albert," she said. "He's awful fast, sometimes. You must mean Albert."

"Sure," said Albert.

The boy looked at him, then shook his head. "He had suspenders," he said. "That's what it looked like anyway. I couldn't see him very well. Listen, we didn't hurt anything, we just wanted to look around, see what it was like is all."

"That all you wanted?" The policeman said they'd talk about that later, and led them to the car, put them into the back seat. They seemed glad to go, Albert thought.

The other policeman shook his head.

"That was the darnedest thing I ever saw," he said. "Looked like someone caught that kid in a flying tackle, except—these two were sitting on the other fellow, I saw them." He rubbed his hand over the top of his head. "I thought I saw them." He gave his head a little shake and grinned. "Anyway, nice work, you guys."

Albert and Brian grinned. The second policeman came back.

"About the dog," he began, and Albert quickly said he must have been afraid of the headlights, must have run away.

"We don't have a dog."

A second police car came, and Mr. Shook said they'd all better get out of the way. "Come on," he said to the boys. "Get your stuff from the tree house."

"You sleeping out? Is that how you heard those guys?" asked the taller policeman. "Nice night for it," he added.

Mr. Shook said it was. "But they'd better finish the night inside."

"They can't do that," Carrie said.

"Why not? Albert has two beds."

"Yes, but—"

Albert interrupted Carrie. "We're sleeping in the tree house. Come on, Brian."

"We are? Now?"

"Of course we are. Our shoes are up there, aren't they?"

Chapter 12

The Only One in the World

The next morning, the policemen came back.

"Are you sure there weren't three of you?" the tall one asked. His name was Patrolman Cutter.

"No, honest, just us," Brian said.

"You went through the building after we went home, didn't you?" asked Albert. "Did you find anyone else?"

"No, but I don't see how you two—I mean, well—" Patrolman Cutter scratched his head. "Those kids insist that there was a boy inside. Were you inside?"

"No. He just got scared by something. You know, all those shadows and then the dog barking. Probably got scared by his own shadow," Albert said.

The policemen said that was it, probably, and they went away again.

Some reporters came and asked questions, too. Albert and Brian were celebrities when the paper came out. Their pictures were on the front page.

Otis didn't come around. Albert couldn't figure out what happened to him. He knew for a fact that he'd beat them to the library the night before. He knew he had scared those kids, and tackled the biggest one. He knew Rags had helped, barking and biting. But neither Otis nor Rags appeared that morning.

In the afternoon, Mr. Harris came. He carried a big box and a newspaper tucked under one arm. He swung his cane and told the boys they had done a good job.

In the back yard, they pulled the packing box out and settled Mr. Harris in his chair, but still Otis did not come.

"He can't be far, we know that," Mr. Harris said. "I have some news for you, anyhow."

"What news?" asked Carrie. She sat crosslegged on the ground at his feet. Brian and Albert leaned against the box.

"I talked to the judge of the Juvenile Court this noon. About those boys." He looked at them soberly. "Seems they admit they did the damage last month, too. They're both at home in the custody of their parents, of course."

Albert nodded. Of course—but that sounded pretty bad to him. He couldn't even imagine what his parents would do, if he ever got into that much trouble.

"Well, the judge thinks he'll sentence them to help move the library from uptown to the new building. They'll have to pack books and unpack them, too."

"That'd be punishment, all right," Brian said.

"Of course, they will still have to pay for the damages. But the judge thinks they should do something good for the library."

Albert thought the boys might never come near the library again, if they had to help move it. Before he could say so, Carrie giggled.

"You're safe now, lazybones," she said to Brian. "You can stop worrying that you'll have to help."

"I hope you're right. But everytime I go in, Mrs. Finch looks as if she's counting my muscles, wondering how many boxes I can carry."

Mr. Harris laughed. "They have a lot of volunteers," he said. "You won't need to help unless you want to. You needn't worry."

"Worry about what?" Otis was suddenly sitting between Albert and Brian, with Rags on his lap. "Who is worried?"

"No one, now. Where have you been?"

"In the library, of course. Those kids had the covers off the paint cans, last night. Did you know that? They were all ready to make a real mess." Otis snapped his suspenders. "I can't abide a mess," he said.

"Don't we know it! Listen, Otis, you did a real good job last night," Albert said. "You scared those kids right out of the building."

"I helped them out, all right. But I wouldn't have known they were there, if you hadn't thrown those stones at the window. I'd have slept all through it."

Otis looked soberly at his friends. "I have to tell you something, Albert. I have to move into the library, after all."

Four pairs of eyes stared at Otis.

Finally, Albert said, "You do?"

"Well, of course I do. That building is going to be the White library, isn't it? It will have all the records of my family in it. Not only that but all the town records, the computer and the copy machine and the TV room—not to mention all those books and magazines. Somebody's got to make sure all that stuff is safe. It stands to reason, Albert, I have to move in there. Why, those kids could have wrecked the whole place last night, if you hadn't heard them. And that's the second time they got in."

"Third," Albert said, and told Otis about the first time, early in the summer.

"Well, then, you see how it is. I wouldn't know what was going on if I kept sleeping in your upper bunk." Otis slapped his knee. "Maybe that's why I'm a ghost, do you think? I'm the last of the Whites. The only one left to watch over the library."

"That could be true," Albert said. "It could be."

"Of course it's true. I've been all over that building, Pud, and you were right. There are a lot of places I could use for Rags and me up on that second floor. One place I like the best, but I wish it had a mattress in it."

"Well," said Mr. Harris. He grinned at Otis.

"Well," said Albert.

"We'll get you a mattress," Carrie said. "We can get an air mattress, can't we? You could blow it up. But what if someone saw it?"

"I'll hide it," Otis said. "But what is an air mattress?"

"You blow it up, like a balloon," Brian said. "We have an extra one at our house, right now."

"Yes, but can a ghost blow up a balloon?" Mr. Harris laughed and answered his own question. "Never mind, if you can't, we'll find a way."

"There's another thing," Otis said, looking sober again. "If I keep looking in those books, maybe I'll find out how long a person stays a ghost."

"Ah, Otis, what do you care how long?" Albert asked.

"Why, Albert, just think of all there is for me to learn yet!" Otis leaned forward, his blue eyes flashing with excitement. "Pud hasn't told half about all those years since nineteen aught-three. I want to find out about the Presidents I missed and all the new things like airplanes and robots and submarines. And there's all those good books to read, and those newspapers, and—"

"That should take you a couple of years right there," Albert said, and the thought of Otis being around that long made him feel happy.

Mr. Harris held out the box he'd brought. "Otis, this is for you," he said. "I meant to use it as a bribe, to get you to move into the library. But I see it had better be a prize, instead, for stopping those boys last night. Go on, open it."

Otis pulled the string and gave it to Rags. The paper fell back from the box, Otis opened the flaps and disappeared.

"Hey!"

"I can't help it, I lost control," Otis explained. "It's the best thing I ever had."

Slowly, out of the big box, came a black transistor radio.

"Gosh almighty," said Otis, and the knob turned and music came out.

Three weeks later the library had its open house. Albert, Carrie and Brian were there early. They wandered about and finally settled at a table in the Children's Room.

"I'll bet this is the only library in the whole world with a ghost and his dog who sleep on an air mattress up under the roof somewhere," Carrie said softly.

"Especially a ghost and his dog listening to the radio every night on that air mattress under the roof," Albert said.

Mrs. Finch came over and smiled at them. "Isn't this a wonderful room?" she asked.

They said it was. They meant it, too. It was sunny and bright and filled with books.

"It has a good feeling about it," she said. "The whole building has a special feeling. I can't explain it."

"A feeling?" Carrie asked, glancing at the boys. Mrs. Finch nodded.

"Remember you boys asked about ghosts this summer? I'll admit, you had me wondering. But this library isn't haunted, at all. Instead, there is a warm, protected feeling. I really cannot explain it," she repeated, and went off to talk to the people coming in the door.

That night Albert went up to his room a little early. School would start the next day, and he didn't feel ready for that. He missed Otis. He couldn't get over expecting Otis to float up and settle onto the upper bunk.

His family didn't miss Otis.

"It was a strange summer," his mother had said at supper, just that night. "So many odd happenings. But things have settled down lately, thank goodness."

"That's true," Mr. Shook said. "The house is warmer, the upstairs radio isn't going all the time." He looked at Albert. "For some reason, I feel the way one does when guests leave, know what I mean? Glad but sad."

"Mmmmmmmmmm," Albert said, his mouth full of spaghetti.

"Well, I still want to know who scratched my favorite record." Sally looked at Albert. He shook his head furiously.

"Not me," he said.

Now, in his room, he kicked his shoes off, dropped his jeans on the floor and tossed his shirt toward the basket. He pulled on his pajamas and opened his new book about bones. He turned one page and then another.

Getting up, he went to the window, and looked toward the dark library. Somewhere, under the roof, Otis was listening to the radio.

"It's all your fault, Otis," he yelled—but softly. Then he picked up his jeans and hung them on a hook. He tossed his shirt into the basket. "I can no longer abide a mess," he said.

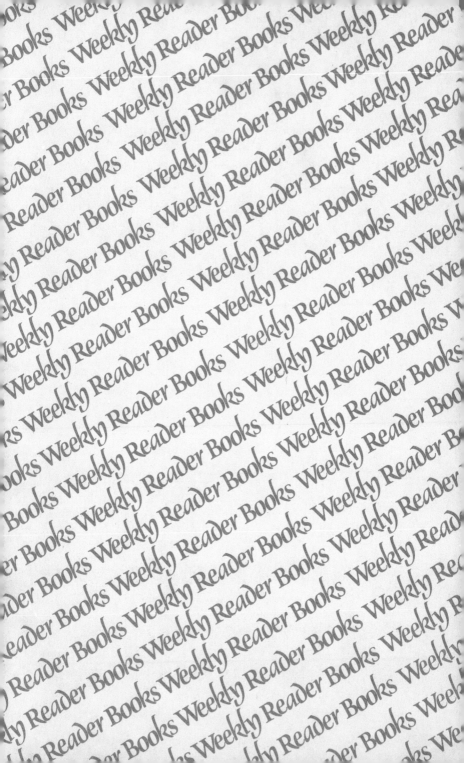